I0534761

Cake, Vows and Extortion

Apple Creek R-Park Department Mysteries

Montie Red

RED

Cover design: MRed

Map Illustrator: M Red

Library of Congress

 Formatted with Vellum

To my biggest and most interesting mystery in life, Josephine

Apple

City Hall

Bakery

Cyder's Pub

Creek

History
Art Museum

Ice Cream&Flower Shop

Chapter 1
Friday, Night time...

The music was the first thing that reached me when I opened the door to the Grand Salon. It had been a very long time since I'd walked into Apple Creek's Country Club wearing a long chiffon evening dress and a fancy hairdo. The last time had been my high school graduation—and my classmates were the ones dancing.

I couldn't help but wonder what my friends from back then would've thought if, just like tonight, I'd walked into the room with my high heels in hand, the seam of my dress half-ripped and muddy, a very sad, limping dog by my side, and a priceless gemstone necklace hidden in my pocket. I mentally thanked myself for having had the sense to choose a dress with hidden pockets.

The last thing I wanted was to cause a scene, so I made my way to the wall, hoping I could spot Officer Tricia from there. Not an easy task, considering Lucy's rehearsal guest list was probably as long as the actual wedding's— three hundred attendees. And I could swear that in the few minutes I'd been gone, the crowd had grown. Apparently, her future in-laws were the kind who mixed business with pleasure. Not for the first time that weekend, I felt like I'd stumbled into a mafia movie.

"Come on, Bruno," I said, glancing down at my sweet and injured companion. When he lifted his front paw, doing his best not to touch the ground, my stomach turned. The necklace in my pocket felt heavier, and I had to swallow the lump in my throat. I should've forced Lucy to involve the police from the start. I was right about her future family, although I'd been wrong about who—and why. Now, it wasn't just intuition anymore. And again, without looking for it, I was involved in the Maple Hollow museum heist.

I kept looking around, but between the dim lighting meant to set the party mood and the fact that my height wasn't exactly basket-ball-approved, the sea of dark suits and long dresses kept blocking my view.

In the back of my mind, I kept thinking about Sandie. I just hoped Paul had reached her and Logan in time.

A hand touched my shoulder, and the only reason I didn't draw attention to myself was because I covered my mouth to muffle a scream.

"Maggie!" Lucy shouted as I turned to her. "What in the world happened to you?" Her eyes traveled down my dress, and disgust spread across her face. "Oh my! You stink!"

I ignored her comment and grabbed her by the shoulders. "Is Logan back? Where's Tricia?"

She rolled her eyes and pushed my hands away. "Don't know. Don't care. He shouldn't even be here." Her voice dropped as she leaned in. "But between you and me, you shouldn't let anyone see you like this. Really. What did you do—jump into a pond?"

Little did she know, her guess wasn't that far off. But that was the least of my problems.

"I need to find either of them," I said. "Where was the last time you—"

A man who, only two days ago, had been a stranger to me walked up behind Lucy. There was a smirk on his face, but the bright purple-and-green bruise under his eye spoke louder—a clear reminder of our recent meeting.

"You have something that belongs to me," he said. His tone had an edge that sliced through the music.

Bruno growled at my side, but I wasn't going to let him get hurt again. I patted his head as gently as I could without taking my eyes off the man.

"Let's take a walk," the man said, slipping an arm around Lucy's waist. She started to pull away, but then froze—her expression flickered as if she'd felt something sharp press lightly against her side, hidden beneath the silk fabric.

Whatever he said to her next was whispered too low for me to hear, but I didn't need the words. I saw the fear in her eyes, and the slight tremble in her shoulders.

"Shall we?" he asked, already steering her toward the exit.

I looked down at Bruno and, as firmly as I could, told him to stay. Maybe if he hadn't been injured, I would've let him act—but not like this.

Then I turned and followed the man and Lucy, wondering how in the world I'd gotten tangled up in all of this.

Chapter 2
Wednesday...

"Unbelievable!" my mom exclaimed from her chair by the kitchen window as she put her phone down. "Did you hear about this?"

I finished rinsing my cup in the sink, still trying to make up for ignoring my alarm that morning. "Hear about what?"

"The heist!"

"A what?" I asked, more concerned about finding my other shoe—and my car keys.

My mom, with all the patience in the world, got up and handed me my purse. "You put your keys in here last night, and Darcy has your shoes."

I looked over at the living room, where my sweet daughter had my mom's purse in one hand, a folded umbrella in the other, wearing one of my jackets—and, of course, my shoes.

"She's just like you," my mom said, following me into the living room.

"Mommy!" Darcy shouted, louder than necessary, as I sat down on the couch. "I'm going to work!"

I smiled at her. "I see that, sunflower—but I kind of need one of the shoes you're wearing."

She looked down at her feet, then at mine. "Well, I didn't know where you put the other one, and I need to wear high heels to the meeting, Mom."

"High heels?" I chuckled, slipping on my barely-one-inch-high shoe.

"Yes, Mom. Those are *super tall* ones."

My mom laughed, leaning against the back of the couch. "Yes, you're practically in stilettos."

Bruno, lounging by the front door, gave a low woof as if to agree, then stretched out long and slow before padding over to inspect Darcy's outfit. He gave her a sniff, then nudged the umbrella with his nose.

I rolled my eyes and changed the topic. "So, what heist were you talking about?"

"Yes! The heist." She stood, looking at her

phone. "I was just reading the article. Apparently, last night during a fundraising event, someone stole a famous necklace. It's made of white gold with several precious stones—but the centerpiece is an alexandrite."

I looked up. "A what?"

She shook her head and brushed her hair back, adopting her best know-it-all tone. "An alexandrite. A very rare gemstone discovered in the Ural Mountains. That's in Russia, Darcy."

Darcy gave her full attention to my mom, who clearly wasn't done.

"They're also found in Tanzania, Sri Lanka, and Brazil, but they're rare anywhere—and they change colors."

"Change colors?" Darcy exclaimed, dropping the umbrella and the purse. "How? Are they magical?"

Bruno cocked his head, clearly intrigued by the shift in energy.

My mom lifted one shoulder and softened her voice, switching into compelling storyteller mode. "The light changes them. In sunlight, it looks bluish or greenish, but under candlelight or a lamp, it turns red. And this one in particular is said to be cursed."

I huffed and got up, walking toward the door. "Mom, really?"

"It's in the article, Maggie," she insisted. "Apparently, all the previous owners had to sell it because they lost their fortunes soon after acquiring it."

"And the new one just lost it completely?" I muttered.

My mom ignored me and turned her attention to her more captivated audience. "You see, Darcy, the last owner—after losing all his money—donated the necklace to the Geology Collection at the Natural Science Museum downtown. He said the necklace had already taken too much from him and he wouldn't let the curse continue. He could've sold it, but no —he just gave it away."

"That was so nice of him," Darcy said. "Do you think the robbers know about the curse? They might be in trouble."

I kissed her forehead as I grabbed my purse. "I think stealing is enough to get someone in trouble, pretty."

"You want to know the crazy part?" my mom said, catching both our attention again. "According to the article, police suspect the thieves took the train first—and they bought tickets to Maple Hollow. But the train broke down, and they escaped on foot." She crossed her arms and grinned. "They think Apple Creek was the most logical route."

Darcy covered her mouth and looked back and forth between us. "Do you think Bruno will be on the case? What if the necklace ended up in our house? I don't want him to get cursed!"

My mom crossed the living room, suddenly concerned, and hugged Darcy. "Oh no, sweetie."

Bruno rushed over, clearly sensing the change in mood, and—true to form—gently but determinedly nudged my mom off balance to plant a big wet kiss on Darcy's cheek.

"Okay, okay," I said, moving in to pull him back a little. "She's safe, detective. At ease."

Just then, the front door burst open and my sister's voice rang out from behind a mountain of flowers and paper bags. "Mom," Sandie called, "can you help with the rest of the bags? We need to start the wedding favors!"

Behind her, her best friend's bouncy curls appeared, along with even more packages.

What followed was twenty straight minutes of rustling tissue paper, misplaced ribbons, half-opened boxes, and mild chaos—Bruno sniffing every single bag as if auditioning for the K9 unit again.

When things finally settled and all the supplies were spread out on the dining table, I slipped quietly into the hallway, purse in hand.

Bruno appeared at my side before I even called him.

"Ready, boy?" I asked as I opened the front door.

He gave one sharp wag of his tail and trotted out ahead of me.

As I backed out of the driveway, I stole a glance in the rearview mirror. Inside, the house was still alive with laughter and wedding chatter.

For the first time that morning, I exhaled. No wedding errands. No bridal drama.

Just me, Bruno, and a quiet shift at the park office.

Or so I thought.

The second I stepped into City Hall, I spotted Linda standing beside Logan, arms crossed and wearing the kind of expression that made my stomach twist.

"What happened?" I asked, trying to

wrestle my overactive imagination into submission. "Is there an—"

"An emergency?" Linda cut in. "Yes, there is an emergency. We have to get to the golf course. Now."

I almost freaked out—until I saw Logan's grin, like he'd just found a bonus cookie. Completely ignoring the sling on his arm. Definitely not a crisis—at least not for him.

"I'll take this guy," he said, giving Bruno's leash a gentle tug. Bruno's tail started wagging as Logan scratched behind his ears. "We've got a less eventful day ahead, buddy."

Linda didn't wait. She grabbed my arm and pulled me toward the door like we were late for a flight. "Come on!"

Logan's grin widened as he called after me, "Good luck, Maggie."

That alone nearly sent me sprinting in the opposite direction.

"Linda, what is going on?"

She sighed as we reached the sidewalk, the kind of sigh that usually came with a migraine. "I'll only say this once." She stopped and turned to face me, her tone suddenly solemn. "Rufus may have been a lot of things, but he was the only one who could deal with Patrick

Potter and his..." she waved her hands in the air like words had failed her, "...eccentricities."

I paused, and for the first time since taking the director job, I had a clear idea of what she meant.

"Pat? Pat Potter? Why do I have to talk to him?"

Linda narrowed her eyes at me like I'd just insulted her mother. "You called him *Pat*?"

"He was my golf coach in high school," I admitted, unlocking my car. "And yes, he's... difficult. But as far as I know, the golf course runs as an enterprise. It's self-sustaining. R-Parks doesn't have to manage it."

"You're correct... partially."

She climbed into the passenger seat without another word. I hesitated for half a second—just long enough to consider hiding in the supply closet—then started the car.

We were halfway out of the parking lot before she continued.

"Patrick Potter is the course manager. Although golf operations are outside the R-Parks department's purview, the clubhouse itself is not. That includes the event space, restaurant, and the bar."

I stopped at the sign just outside City Hall and stared at her.

"You're telling me the building isn't part of the enterprise?"

"Exactly." Her expression softened, but only slightly. "The golf course is *his* business. The building is *ours*."

I felt the temperature in the car drop. The last thing we needed was to babysit an event center mid-wedding season. After the chaos of the spring festival, the paperwork mountain on my desk had started to look almost manageable —until now.

"What happened?" I asked, knowing I wouldn't like the answer.

"He fired the caterer."

I blinked. "But... you just said he's not in charge of the clubhouse."

"He shouldn't be," Linda snapped. "But he did. And the caterer is gone. I tried to talk to them, but..."

I pressed my foot harder on the gas without realizing it. "Maybe I can convince them to come back. The last thing they want is to lose all their summer contracts. They must have tons of graduations and—"

I stopped.

Lucy's wedding.

Thursday dinner. Friday rehearsal. Saturday wedding. Sunday brunch.

Sandie's long explanation about themes, menus, and hand-lettered seating charts came flooding back like a second tidal wave.

Linda must have seen the realization hit me because she didn't even give me a chance to speak.

"According to Pat, he already found the *perfect* replacement."

I gripped the steering wheel and shook my head. "That cannot be good."

"Exactly!" Linda said, hands flying up in exasperation. And then, more quietly, with a note of genuine frustration, she added, "Pat can't get his way on this, Margaret. Someone needs to put him in his place. This department needs to be respected by everyone in that course."

I didn't answer. I knew this wouldn't end well.

Chapter 3

"**M**aggie!" Patrick Potter shouted from the back of the clubhouse as Linda and I walked inside. "Or should I say *Margaret*, now that you run the R-Parks Department?"

I smiled, not missing the sarcasm. Thanks to Linda, I'd just found out why Pat always thought the city—especially our department—was poorly run. Over the years, while I was training with him, he never hesitated to share his opinions about the country club.

"Pat, I knew you weren't a fan of the country club, but don't you think the golfers might miss food and drinks after a round?"

His smug grin didn't budge, but his eyes narrowed. He hated being called Pat by people he didn't consider equals. I was sure he'd prefer "Mr. Potter" from me, his former student.

"There's nothing to worry about," he said, waving us forward down the hallway. "I've got it all sorted."

The country house had once been a stuffy, carpeted mansion, but back during my pregnancy with Darcy, it had been fully renovated —light walls, clean wood floors, and big windows replaced the gloomy, dark interior. The restaurant was now an open, sunlit space with patio seating and a modern bar.

"Nico!" Pat called as we entered. "Come meet someone!"

From behind the bar popped a tan guy with a bright smile and a towel over his shoulder. "Meet someone? I thought I was here to fix this place, not make friends."

"You mean in a couple of days," Pat replied with a grin. "And you'll want to meet your boss."

Nico looked from Linda to me, confused. "Wait—boss? I thought you said *you* were in charge, Pat."

I crossed my arms and raised an eyebrow. "Of course he did."

Pat chuckled. "Technically, I'm the one who keeps the lights on. This place bleeds money, and I'm the only one willing to make hard choices."

I turned to Nico, who at least didn't look amused. "And you are?"

"Sorry—Nicholas Henson. Most folks call me Nico." He reached to shake my hand. "I've run my family's catering company for years. Pat was... in a bind. I didn't mean to overstep."

"I'm Margaret Willow, Director of Recreation and Parks. This course and clubhouse are city-owned. Pat doesn't hire or fire anyone on his own."

"Understood," Nico said. "I admire what the city's done here. Public access, great condition—it's why I was heading this way, actually."

"Heading this way?" Linda asked.

Nico nodded. "Yeah. I was supposed to take the train to Maple Hollow this week—had some meetings lined up. But with the breakdown, plans shifted, and Pat reached out. I figured I'd stop by and lend a hand."

Linda and I exchanged a look. A broken train, a detour, and suddenly Pat's new favorite caterer? Too convenient.

"Well, let's hear your pitch," I said. "You're here now."

Nico exhaled. "Right. I can show you what

we do. Farm-to-table, flexible menu, all licensed and staffed. We've handled weddings, galas, even state events—"

"Perfect!" Pat cut in. "He's the answer. We'll finally have real food again."

"Pat," I said sharply, "that's not your call to make. Should I start hiring golf coaches without asking you?"

He smirked—until I added, "Because I *am* your boss."

Pat's mouth snapped shut.

Turning back to Nico, I softened my tone. "I don't know you or your business, but I do know we've got a major wedding this weekend. Can you handle that?"

"A wedding? This weekend?" Nico said, then regained his footing. "Absolutely. I can cater the event."

"And a welcome dinner, rehearsal, and post-wedding brunch," Linda added, arms crossed.

Nico hesitated only a second. "Yes. We can do all of it."

"Do you have experience running a restaurant and bar?" I asked.

He looked down, and his silence answered for him.

"Then we'll treat this catering event as your

trial run," I said. "Let's see what you can do before we finalize a contract."

"What about the restaurant?" Pat said, arms folded and scowling.

"We're closing it," I said, trying to think fast. "At least for today—maybe tomorrow."

"What?" Pat raised his voice. "You can't! The course is booked solid!"

"Then maybe you should've thought of that before firing the caterer."

I turned on my heel and walked out.

"This is unacceptable!" Pat shouted after us. "This is *your* problem now!"

"It is," I said, not stopping. "And it's closed. For sure until tomorrow."

"Then what?"

I didn't even look back. "Then you'll see."

Linda didn't speak until we were in the car.

"Tomorrow? Do you actually have a plan?"

I smiled like I did. She wasn't fooled.

Linda groaned. "Great."

And that's when it hit me: I had no plan. Not yet. But the countdown had already started.

"I need to talk to Terry," I said to Linda as we walked into the office.

I hadn't heard anything about this Nicholas Henson or his family business, but Terry had managed the food section during the Art Festival. If there was anything to know about them, Terry would've heard it.

However, when I opened my office door, I found my sister Sandie and her best friend Lucy waiting for me.

"So sorry, boss," Bert said, rushing toward me from the other side of the department. "I tried to catch you, but I was on the phone."

His apologetic smile didn't help much, but there was nothing I could do. Sandie's expression said she meant business, and Lucy's sobs were steadily increasing in volume.

"Hey," I said, walking in and doing my best to pretend I didn't know anything—though I had a pretty good idea of what was happening. As the bride, Lucy must've just heard from her caterer that they wouldn't be working her wedding anymore. I knew this was coming; I just wished I'd had more time to find a proper solution.

"This is bad, Maggie," Sandie said.

I agreed with her, though I didn't get the chance to say anything before Lucy burst out:

"It's a nightmare! I can't believe my mother-in-law could be such a— I know it's important to the family, but that doesn't mean she can threaten my future. My *marriage!*"

I frowned, trying to understand. "Your mother-in-law threatened—?"

"Yes!" Lucy threw her arms up and began pacing around my office, her sobs and choppy words making it hard to follow. "And I didn't even want to wear that stupid necklace. It totally clashed with my dress and accessories, but no—she insisted. Said it was a family tradition, some historical heirloom, or whatever. She was just using it to get rid of me!"

I narrowed my eyes and looked at Sandie, whose expression was tight with agreement.

"I'm sorry, Lucy," I said. "An heirloom? What exactly is going on?"

Lucy collapsed into the chair in front of my desk and buried her face in her hands, which made it nearly impossible to hear her.

"I lost Johnathan's family heirloom last night," she mumbled. "Well—not lost. It was stolen."

I didn't know much about Lucy's fiancé, but I did know his family was wealthy—and apparently a big deal in Maple Hollow, where the Cullens had lived for decades, maybe even centuries.

"If someone stole the necklace, you need to call the—"

"No!" Lucy jumped up and slammed her hands on my desk. "I can't call the police. I can't tell anyone. If she finds out, I'll lose Johnathan!"

"Why would you lose Johnathan?" I asked, genuinely confused. Shouldn't love be stronger than a lost piece of jewelry?

"Because she'll take him away from me!"

"Who?"

At the same time, Lucy and Sandie shouted a name that would be engraved in my memory forever.

"Dorothy Cullens!"

Lucy slowly sat back down, her sobs making it hard for her to speak again.

Sandie stepped closer to her friend and gently rubbed her back. "Mrs. Cullens is the head of the family," she said with a shake of her head. "You've seen gangster movies—you know what being the head means."

I had seen several movies about powerful families and crime bosses, and I was certain I wouldn't want to get mixed up with any of them. But this was Sandie and Lucy. They did have a flair for the dramatic.

"So you think this woman will send an assassin after Lucy over a necklace? Oh wait—was it the one that got stolen last night at the gala in the city?"

Sandie frowned at me. "Of course not, Maggie. But just because this necklace isn't worth millions doesn't mean it's not important. And no, I don't think Lucy's in physical danger, but Mrs. Cullens could intervene and cancel the wedding."

"She can't do that," I said, truly believing it —which only made Lucy cry harder.

"Oh, she *can*," my sister said, her expression shifting between exasperated and heartbroken. "Johnathan's a mama's boy."

Lucy looked up, trying to defend him. "He's not that bad... he just hates upsetting his mom."

Again, I wondered why anyone would want to marry under those conditions—but who was I to judge?

"All right," I said. "What are you going to do, then?"

Lucy wiped her eyes carefully to avoid smudging her mascara and took a deep breath. "Sandie told me you're good at investigating things. I—we were hoping you could help me find it."

I stepped back, probably looking as shocked as I felt. Sandie took that as her cue to pile on.

"You're great at solving cases! Sure, the painting wasn't found, but you found the killer. This is just a thief—we're talking piece of cake." She smiled like she truly believed it.

"I'm not a detective," I said, looking Lucy straight in the eyes. "And you really should call the police. If the necklace is insured, they'll need a report—"

Lucy reached out and grabbed my hand. "I *can't* lose Johnathan. That witch warned me this would happen. She made it very clear she didn't want me marrying her son. I think she used someone from the wedding party to take it. Please, Maggie. If I call the police, she wins. This was supposed to be the wedding of my dreams. And now... please."

Maybe it was the guilt from knowing our golf manager had already accidentally ruined part of her wedding—and she didn't even know it yet—but the moment I nodded, two sets of arms wrapped around me in a tight hug.

"But," I said once I'd untangled myself,

"we need to talk about your plans for the week."

Both women stepped back as I tried to smile and make things sound better than they were.

"Funny story," I said. "There's been a development at the country club. You might want to sit back down for this one."

Chapter 4

Probably because I agreed to help with the necklace, Lucy didn't murder me—but she made it very clear how displeased she was about the whole situation, especially since the country club had suddenly become my top priority.

"You wanted to see me?" Terry said from the doorway of my office.

It was funny how this older, bulky guy—who'd had more accidents in the department than the rest of us combined—had suddenly become my last hope.

"Terry, please come in."

His face paled as he stepped inside gingerly, so I added quickly, "You're not in trouble. I am."

He sat down with more confidence—until

he accidentally knocked over a pencil holder, and I barely managed to save the tiny cactus my mom and Darcy had gifted me for my desk.

"I'm so sorry, Maggie. I was just trying to—"

"No need to worry, Terry," I said, kneeling to collect the pens before he could hurt himself. The last thing I needed was another injury this week. "Did Linda fill you in on what's happening with the country club?"

Terry nodded as I took my seat again.

"It's unacceptable," he said. "Potter shouldn't be messing with our part of the golf course. He's already taken enough."

I tilted my head, surprised by how personal he sounded, and debated whether I should ask —but then he kept talking, and the moment passed.

"She also told me about the other guy. Henson."

"Did you hear anything about him or his business during the Art Festival planning?"

Terry shook his head. "I wasn't really looking into catering companies. I focused more on the local food vendors."

A twist of unease settled in my stomach. "Do you think you could ask around? See if anyone's heard of him—or the so-called family business?"

"Of course. But Maggie..." He hesitated. "If Potter found him, that tells me Henson's probably a golfer. You might want to ask around that crowd, too. I'm not really in that circle."

His eyes dropped, and for a moment I thought I saw something—pain? Regret?— flicker behind them. But it wasn't my place to pry.

"That's a good idea," I said. "I'll follow up on that. Just let me know if you hear anything."

"What are you going to do about the restaurant?" he asked.

I sighed. "Not sure yet. Do you have any ideas?"

Terry chuckled and shook his head. "I'm no expert in the food industry. I just enjoy eating. Too bad Detective Forest's parents are in Florida—they were real pros in that field."

A spark of hope lit up in my chest as I stood. "Terry, you're a genius. I need to talk to an expert."

As I stepped out into the hallway, Linda handed me a printed photo. It showed a group of girls in matching pajamas, all beaming at the camera. The one in the center wore a wedding veil—and a large necklace around her neck. The pendant was hard to make out, except for the fact that it was enormous. Too big for my taste.

"Your sister made me promise not to let you leave without this," Linda said.

I exhaled and took the paper from her. The food expert would have to wait.

First, I needed to talk to a different kind of specialist—someone in a field I knew almost nothing about.

I'd been in Logan's office before, but this was the first time I found him actually behind his desk—neat, organized, and looking oddly focused... on teaching Bruno a trick.

"Getting bored?" I asked.

He chuckled and tossed a treat. Bruno caught it midair, then bounded over to me, tail wagging like a metronome on overdrive. I crouched to greet him, smiling as he leaned against me, all warmth and wagging fluff.

"Maggie," Logan said, turning in his chair.

Seeing his arm still in a sling punched a

small, familiar hole in my stomach. Even if I'd just seen him that morning—I still hated it.

"You know he's working, right?" Logan said, pointing to Bruno's vest. "No pampering on duty."

I ignored the warning and took a seat across from him. "How are you feeling?"

He lifted his slinged arm a few inches. "This? The doctor's being dramatic. I'll be back at work soon enough."

"Looks like you've been busy." I tapped the polished desk. "I didn't even know this thing was dark wood."

He laughed—that rare sound I liked more than I wanted to admit. "Turns out time moves really slow when you're benched. But I assume you're not here to admire furniture—or to pick up Bruno early. What's going on?"

I hesitated. "I have a hypothetical question."

He leaned back and raised an eyebrow. "Hypothetical. That's never a good sign."

"Just tell me how you'd investigate a theft."

He squinted at me. "You taking notes now?"

Caught, I opened my mouth—then closed it. He handed me a pen and notepad from the tidy desk.

"It's simple," he said in that calm, cop-voice tone that meant I needed to brace myself. "You pull out your phone and call the police."

I tossed the pen down. "Logan!"

"No, Maggie." His voice sharpened. "You need to stay away from that heist."

"Heist? What are you talking about?"

"You really expect me to believe it's a coincidence that you're asking about a theft the same morning the biggest heist in the county happens?"

"This isn't about that!" I protested. "It's not even close!"

He leaned forward. "And the fact it happened right around the corner from your old job—also a coincidence?"

I blinked. "Wait—you know where I used to work?"

He ran a hand through his hair, ignoring the question. "Not the point. This crew is serious. Organized-crime-level serious. You can't go sniffing around."

I crossed my arms. "You think I'm that nosy?"

"Yes."

"Maybe someone's stealing office supplies! Ever consider that?"

He arched a brow. "Staples? That's your big case?"

"Do you know how much companies lose each year to theft like that? Probably... dozens of dollars!"

He sighed and gave me a long, steady look. "Are you really here because of staples?"

I sighed too and gave up the charade. "Lucy lost an heirloom. A necklace. *Not* the necklace. Just... an important one. Her future mother-in-law is threatening to cancel the wedding if it's not found by Saturday."

He exhaled deeply and settled back in his chair. "Of course."

"She thinks someone at the bachelorette party took it. And she doesn't want to involve the police because she's terrified of her fiancé's mom. Apparently, he's no help because she rules his life like a dictator in pearls."

Logan rubbed his chin and stared at the wall. For a second, I forgot what I was saying—because I realized we were talking about his ex. And just like that, all the warm fluttery feelings in my stomach turned into cold, jealous ones.

"If it weren't Lucy, I'd think you were making it up," he finally said, smiling faintly. "Check her luggage. Her room. Call the train's lost and found. Lucy has a tendency to misplace things and blame everyone else."

I opened my mouth to defend her—when Arthur knocked and barreled into the office.

"Maggie!" he exclaimed, far too excited. "Brilliant move bringing her in, Logan!"

Logan groaned.

"Bringing me into what?" I asked warily.

"The heist!" Arthur said, closing the door behind him. "You and me, Logan. We'll solve it. Quietly, of course."

I turned to Logan, arms crossed and in full mom-glare mode. He sank lower in his chair and looked to the ceiling for strength.

"Arthur. She's not here for that."

Arthur blinked. "Oh. Upsy."

Logan let out a long breath and then looked at me, resigned. "Fine. I'll help you. But only on one condition."

I raised a brow. "Which is?"

He pointed at Bruno, who was happily chewing on a toy under the desk. "He stays with you. Full-time. Until I'm back on duty. You're his temporary handler."

Bruno's ears perked up. He trotted over and leaned against my leg again, as if already agreeing to the terms.

"Deal," I said.

Montie Red

Bruno barked once—clearly satisfied.

Chapter 5

As I drove toward Cyder's Pub, the windows down, the breeze warm and familiar, I glanced at Bruno in the passenger seat. His nose was up, tongue out, ears flapping in the wind like a dog version of a kite.

"You think I'm a bad influence on Logan?" I asked.

Bruno gave a soft huff, unbothered, as usual.

"Right? I mean, sure, he tossed me out of his office, but he'll hear from me again about that unauthorized heist Arthur and he are working on. I just don't want him getting into real trouble—the dangerous kind."

Bruno sneezed dramatically in response, which I chose to interpret as a "focus, Maggie" kind of gesture.

"Fine, fine. Bigger fires to put out," I said, pulling into the small lot behind Cyder's Pub. "Come on, let's hope Mr. Elliot has a secret restaurant manager hidden in the back. And maybe a chicken sandwich for you."

Bruno trotted at my side, his vest on but his tail still wagging. Inside, the pub had its usual Tuesday crowd: a few retired regulars playing cards, a couple of guys at the bar pretending not to watch the sports rerun on TV, and at least one person I thought might be my mother hiding behind a menu.

Before I could look twice, the swinging kitchen door opened and Mr. Elliot stepped out carrying a large box, followed closely by a younger man with two more.

"Maggie!" he called, setting the box down. "And Bruno! This brightens the day."

Bruno took that as permission and padded toward him, tail in full helicopter mode. Mr. Elliot chuckled and gave him a pat on the head.

"Felix!" he called over his shoulder. "Come meet someone."

The younger man—late twenties, athletic build, black T-shirt, and sleeves of tattoos like abstract art—carefully set his boxes down and came over. His smile was confident, but it had a warmth that made him instantly likable.

"Maggie, this is my nephew, Felix Colling-wood. He's helping out around here until the end of the year. Poor kid got stuck with his old uncle."

Felix extended a hand. "Not stuck at all. I'm grateful to be here."

"Margaret Willow," I said, shaking his hand. "Welcome to Apple Creek."

His grin widened. "Thanks! I haven't been here since I was five, but I always remembered it being... well, cozier."

Mr. Elliot looked down at the floor at that, the smile slipping just enough to suggest something unsaid. I didn't press.

"If you want a tour of the parks, let me know," I offered.

"She's our Parks Director," Mr. Elliot added proudly. "And her mom is probably why we sell out of our chowder twice a week."

I laughed. "That's not an exaggeration."

Felix pointed down to Bruno, now sitting obediently next to my leg.

"And who's this gentleman?"

"This is Bruno," I said. At his name, Bruno perked up. "The best K-9 officer in the department. And a sucker for belly rubs."

Felix crouched to offer a hand. Bruno gave it a good sniff and finished with a polite tail thump, which, to me, meant Felix passed inspection.

"Well," Mr. Elliot said, giving Bruno a fond scratch, "what can I do for you, Maggie? Something to eat? Or something else?"

I sighed. "I've got a problem at the Country Club. Think we can talk?"

He nodded and motioned to a booth in the corner. "Felix, finish sorting those bottles. I'll be right over here."

Once we were seated, he folded his hands on the table. "Hit me."

"We lost our caterer this morning. No manager, no staff. Nothing."

Mr. Elliot let out a low whistle. "That's a mess. What happened?"

"Patrick Potter."

"Say no more," he muttered, rubbing his forehead. "Pat's... well. Let's just say the man's ego could sink a cruise ship."

"You remember he used to coach golf at the high school, right?"

"Oh sure. You were on the team too, weren't you?" His face softened with the memory. "I used to play back in the day—nothing serious, but I enjoyed it."

"Why'd you stop?"

He lifted his leg slightly and patted his

knee. "That, and too many people telling me I had a swing like a broken umbrella."

I chuckled. "Relatable. Life gets in the way."

"You were better than you give yourself credit for," he said, pointing at me. "And rumor has it, Pat's lost his edge lately. Just sayin'."

That gave me pause. "You think so?"

"Heard it from two guys who've played with him. He's been overcompensating—more aggressive, blaming his caddie. Could be something to it."

"That's interesting. I'll have to check on it. But first, I need someone who can help me keep the restaurant running. Just for a few days while I sort this mess with the council and hopefully hire someone new."

He scratched his jaw, frowning. "I'd offer Felix, but he's got energy, not experience. Maybe Agnes?"

"Mrs. O'Leary?"

"She bakes for half the town. Knows everyone who's ever cooked or served a plate around here."

"I'll check in with her," I said, hopeful for the first time all day.

"One more thing," I added, sliding out of

the booth. "Have you ever heard of a Nicholas Henson? He says his family has a catering business in Maple Hollow."

Mr. Elliot made a face. "Can't say I've met him, but long ago I heard a caterer from Maple Hollow used to throw big parties up by the lake. Never paid vendors on time. Bit of a charmer. Could be the same guy."

If this was Nico, I didn't like his reputation. Despite being rumors, it was more information than I'd had previously. With this, I could have another conversation with Pat.

"Thanks," I said, then turned to Bruno, who was sitting politely next to the bar. His eyes were locked on a half-eaten sandwich someone had abandoned two stools down.

"Don't even think about it," I whispered.

Bruno sighed audibly, like the world's most underappreciated detective.

Mr. Elliot gave me a wave. "Good luck, Maggie. And let me know what Agnes says."

As we stepped out into the golden evening light, I scratched behind Bruno's ears and glanced toward the hills where the Country

Club sat like a smug old mansion waiting to ruin someone's week.

"I know I said I'd deal with the missing heirloom," I murmured, "but I need to find out if Nico Henson is involved in dirty business. And fast."

Bruno woofed once in agreement, tail swishing low and ready.

We had a wedding to save—and maybe, just maybe, a thief to catch.

As I opened the door to O'Leary's Creamery, the sweet scent of vanilla and waffle cones wrapped around me like a hug. For a moment, I almost forgot about the mess at the Country Club. Almost.

Bruno padded in beside me, nose twitching, eyes alert. He sniffed toward the glass case with practiced discretion—he'd learned early that drooling on the display was frowned upon.

If Felix could help even a little, maybe I just needed someone else to run the kitchen. I had to check in with the servers too, but that felt like the least of my problems at the moment.

A teen girl behind the counter—probably a high schooler—looked up from a half-melted swirl she was scooping and gave Bruno a curious smile.

"What can I get for you?" she asked, brushing her bangs out of her face.

"I'm looking for Mrs. O'Leary," I said.

Her eyes widened slightly, and she disappeared through the back door. Less than a minute later, Mrs. O'Leary herself emerged with the same energy she used to deliver gossip, pies, and firm advice.

"Maggie! You're not the Willow girl I usually see around this time."

I raised an eyebrow. "How often does Darcy come here?"

"Oh, sweetie, I was talking about your mother," she laughed, waving me toward the patio. "Darcy is just her adorable excuse. Sometimes she brings your daughter, sometimes your sweet nephew Toby. Either way, someone always leaves with sprinkles."

Noted. My mom was apparently running a sugar smuggling operation. Darcy and I were going to have a little talk—and she owed me at least two cones' worth of restitution.

"Mrs. O'Leary," I said, as we walked past the pastel booths to the sun-drenched patio, "I may need your help with something very important."

Her eyes sparkled with curiosity. "Well, that sounds exciting. Let's sit where the sun can do its job."

Bruno was already one step ahead of us. He'd sprawled in a perfect sunbeam, stretched out like a very furry rug, blinking slowly in contentment. He looked so peaceful, I considered laying down beside him and pretending the world didn't exist for just five minutes.

"What kind of trouble are we talking, Maggie?" she asked, settling into a wrought-iron chair with floral cushions.

I filled her in—the abrupt firing of the catering company, the now-chaotic state of the Country Club's restaurant, and Mr. Elliot offering Felix's help.

She listened carefully, her brow furrowed but not surprised. When I finished, she let out a soft sigh.

"I swear, Pat Potter could cause a ruckus in a monastery," she muttered. "My son Larry's back in town. He is looking for a job, and—he's a wonderful cook, could help in the kitchen. But managing a restaurant? That's another thing altogether."

I felt the hopeful spark fizzle a bit, but

nodded anyway. "Do you think if I find someone who can run the place, Larry might be willing to fill in for at least a couple of weeks?"

"Oh, absolutely," she said. Then her tone softened as she leaned across the table and gently held my hands. "But Maggie... this isn't your mess to clean up. This is Pat's. He needs to be held accountable."

I nodded slowly. "I agree with you. Linda does too. She's worried about what'll happen if we just let him steamroll over the venue. He's already acting like he owns the place."

"He's been puffed up too long," Mrs. O'Leary said. "Troy gave him too much rope, and now the man thinks he's invincible. It won't stop unless someone pushes back."

"I'm not letting him ruin that restaurant," I said, sitting back. "But I also need it to survive the next few weeks while I talk to the mayor and the council."

She gave my hands a final squeeze. "You'll figure it out. You're more resourceful than you think."

Bruno gave a soft woof, as if to second the motion. He stood, stretched with an exaggerated yawn, and padded over to rest his head on my foot.

I smiled. "Thanks, Mrs. O'Leary. I'll call you soon—if Larry's still available, I might just take you up on it."

"Best of luck, Maggie," she said as I stood. "And maybe bring Darcy next time. I'll even throw in a cone for you—butter pecan?"

I grinned as Bruno and I stepped out into the late afternoon sun. "Deal."

As we walked back toward the car, I glanced down at Bruno. "We've almost patched the catering hole, but... I still think there's more to Nico's family business. And I haven't forgotten about that heirloom. Let's hope Arthur and Logan have been more successful with the heist."

Bruno looked up, ears twitching.

"I know," I said. "We've got a wedding to save."

Chapter 6

I didn't need to listen to my sister's voicemail. I already knew what it would say—and probably how loud it would be. Instead, I drove straight to the house where Lucy was staying before the wedding.

Though Lucy lived in Apple Creek, Sandie had told me she wanted the entire wedding party and immediate family under one roof for the week. She claimed it was for bonding and convenience, but we all knew the truth: it was the only way she could keep everyone on schedule for her master plan of bridal perfection.

As we pulled up to the rented house, Bruno sat upright in the passenger seat, ears perked, nose twitching.

"Fancy," I muttered, eyeing the massive

white home that looked more like a movie set than a rental. "Think they have a treat bar inside?"

Bruno responded with a low *wuff*, as if deeply skeptical.

The house looked as big—maybe bigger—than Mrs. Catherine Roberts' estate, perched on the opposite end of the golf course. Apple Creek wasn't exactly a tourist hotspot, but its riverside charm and quiet atmosphere made it the kind of place where people from the city came to breathe, celebrate, and pretend their lives were simpler.

Before I could knock, the door burst open.

"There you are!" Sandie shouted, dragging me inside by the arm. "Lucy's been losing her mind. Did you figure out anything?"

Bruno followed right on my heels, his claws clicking softly against the pristine wood floor as he paused to sniff the entryway rug, then the decorative baskets near the door, clearly cataloging the scent chaos.

I didn't answer right away. The interior of the house was gorgeous—modern lines, soft neutral tones, high ceilings—but wedding prep had swallowed the décor up. Tulle, favor boxes, and scattered flower petals covered every surface. Bruno eyed a toppled vase suspiciously before carefully sidestepping it.

"What happened here?" I asked, lifting a soggy scrap of tulle that had drooped into a flowerless vase.

"Lucy," Sandie groaned, rubbing her belly, now impressively round. "She's been tearing the place apart. Looked for the necklace last night, again this morning, and then again an hour ago."

From the back of the house came the unmistakable sound of shrieking laughter and what might've been a cannonball splash.

Bruno tilted his head and turned in that direction.

"Wedding party," Sandie said, flopping down onto a couch covered in lavender fabric and buried under at least ten pillows. "Most of the groomsmen are Johnathan's cousins, plus some friends—ten of them in total. Lucy's bridesmaids are a mix of his cousins, two of our high school friends, Lauren and Sonia, and me. With this giant baby as my plus-one."

Bruno took this as an invitation and walked over to Sandie, gently resting his chin on her knee. Her features softened immediately as she scratched behind his ears.

"I am exhausted," she added, smiling down

at him. "You're the only guy around here who understands me, Bruno."

He licked her hand gently, then laid down at her feet like a loyal throw rug with a badge.

I found a spot on the opposite couch, moving aside what looked like boxes of lavender sachets. "How are you feeling? You look—well, you look like you've been through a wedding week."

"I love Lucy," Sandie said, eyes half-lidded, "but I may throttle her. Everyone else is just here for the free cake. It's like I'm the only one who actually cares about this wedding."

A fresh round of laughter and a splash echoed from the back.

Sandie winced. "See? A bunch of irresponsible adults pretending they're in college again. I know Johnathan's younger than Lucy, but come on   he's not a teenager."

Bruno let out a soft, disgruntled *whuff*, like he was equally unimpressed.

"I wanted to say you're starting to sound like a mom," I teased, "but you're right."

"I am a mom," she muttered, then gave up trying to reposition the pillows and let herself sink into them like a disgruntled marshmallow. "Lucy's been upstairs. Ever since we left your office, she has been tearing rooms apart. I think someone really took that necklace, Maggie."

That made me pause. Sandie knew Lucy better than Logan. If she was sure, Logan's idea was out the window.

Sandie let out a big breath before she continued describing the picture to me. "Closets, drawers, even the vents. I caught her tapping walls like she was in a spy movie."

"I assume your voicemail was about her?"

Sandie tilted her head and narrowed her eyes at me. "You didn't listen to it?"

"I figured I'd get the live performance."

"Why do I bother?" she grumbled. "Yes. I called because she's spiraling. I tried to help, but I need a break. A bubble bath. Silence. Maybe a babysitter for my own brain."

I patted her leg gently. "You stay right here. I'll talk to her. Maybe we can get her to take a breath before she flips the whole house upside down."

Bruno, already back on his feet, trotted to my side with purpose, tail wagging low and slow.

"Good luck," Sandie muttered as I made my way to the staircase.

"Come on, partner," I said to Bruno.

He gave a little snort, as if to say *about time*,

and led the way up the stairs, nose twitching with every step—his detective instincts clearly on high alert.

Sandie hadn't been exaggerating.

Lucy was in full paranoia mode when I walked into the main bedroom upstairs. She stood mid-swing, about to hurl a large vase of white roses at the wall.

"Wait up!" I lunged forward, steadying the vase in her hands. "Do you really think the necklace is in there?"

Lucy exhaled loudly, allowing me to set the vase gently on a table at the center of the room. I surveyed the space, blinking. If the rest of the house looked like chaos, this room was a five-alarm disaster. It brought to mind the vandalized warehouse before the art festival—but with significantly more tulle.

Bruno padded in behind me, nose twitching as he sniffed around the room. He paused at a corner near an overturned shoebox, ears perking, then moved to inspect the bed's edge like a detective silently taking mental notes.

"I know how it looks, Maggie," Lucy said, flopping into a chair by the balcony. "I'm not crazy. I just need to find it. I shouldn't have agreed to keep it, but Dorothy insisted—and no one says no to her."

I began tidying as I walked—more for my sanity than hers. For once, I almost hoped it *had* been stolen. Finding anything in here would be like hunting a pearl in a tidepool after a hurricane.

"I have to ask," I said, glancing back at her. "Are you sure it was taken?"

Tears slid down Lucy's cheeks. "I lose things, I know I do—but not this. I barely even touched it. I took it out for the photos Dorothy wanted, then put it right back in the box."

I didn't need to ask—she was already pointing toward the closet. "The box is there. Empty."

I opened the door to reveal what seemed like the biggest walk-in closet imaginable. It looked more like a boutique changing room, complete with an island of drawers and a fresh flower arrangement.

"This is the size of my bedroom," I muttered.

Lucy actually chuckled, which felt like a

small victory. "I know. It was perfect—until it wasn't."

She walked to the drawer island and opened the top one, revealing a small safe with a digital number lock. "I put the box in here before dinner. When I got back, it was open—and empty."

"I don't think Johnathan's going to cancel the wedding over a necklace," I said softly, moving closer. "He loves you. An heirloom shouldn't matter more than you do."

She looked at me, eyes rimmed with red. "Maybe he won't—but how do we recover from this? His mom already doesn't like me. This is just going to prove her right. I don't want to start our life with drama and shame."

That, at least, I could understand. Bruno sat quietly near Lucy, watching her like he understood too. She absently reached down and scratched his head.

"I get why you don't want to go to the police," I said. "But maybe we talk to a detective. Off the record. Logan knows how to handle situations like this."

Lucy stiffened. "I'm not talking to him. I've accepted the fact that your family is cozying up to him again because of that adorable puppy—no offense, Bruno—but I'm not forgiving him."

I exhaled through my nose. "Lucy, Logan *did* invite you to prom."

Her eyes narrowed. "That was barely an invitation."

I paused, feeling the tension spike. This wasn't really about prom. This was pressure, fear, heartbreak—all bubbling over. Still, it was hard not to roll my eyes.

"He asked you on the way home from practice—sure, it was casual. But that doesn't mean it wasn't real."

"He didn't even ask, Maggie! He said, 'I guess we should go to prom.' *Guess?!* What was I supposed to say? I had plans, ideas—it was supposed to be special. He ruined that for me."

I swallowed my rising frustration. "His mom was in chemotherapy. They didn't even know if she'd make it."

"I knew that," she whispered, turning toward the window. "But I just wanted one night where he forgot about it. One night that could still feel normal."

"And when he didn't give you the fantasy version, you cut him out completely?" I asked. "That seems like a big reaction for someone who was thinking of him."

Lucy's lips parted, then closed. Her voice, when it returned, was softer. "He broke my heart. And now you want me to hand that same heart to him and ask for help?"

I let the silence settle, then gently said, "I think he'd be happy to help."

"No," she said firmly. "If you want to help me, fine. But I don't want him involved—and definitely not the police."

I pressed my hands over my face for a moment, trying to steady the frustration brewing behind my eyes. Before I could speak, Lucy added—

"I want what you and Sandie have—a family. Sure, maybe Andrew's gone, but you have Darcy. I have nothing yet, and this is my third engagement. I can't fail again. If the necklace isn't found by the rehearsal, I'll talk to Johnathan and his mom. But until then... please help me."

She was shaking. Not angry now—just scared.

Bruno gently bumped her leg with his head, almost like he was saying, *We've got this.* How could I say no to that?

"All right," I said softly. "Do you suspect anyone?"

Chapter 7

According to Lucy, there were two suspects.

One was a cousin from Johnathan's side of the groom's party, Louis Cullens. He'd been fascinated by the necklace during the shoot, excitedly discussing the gems and a near-disaster at his sister's wedding where she almost lost it in a lake. She also claimed he adored Dorothy Cullens, the future mother-in-law, and would "do anything for her," though given Lucy's description of the woman, I mentally filed that under *highly biased*. Still, worth checking out.

The other was Melody Carter, a distant cousin and one of her bridesmaids. Lucy had only invited her to keep the wedding aesthetic —ten bridesmaids and ten groomsmen. They'd met at holidays and weddings, and Lucy insisted Melody had always been jealous—borrowing clothes, jewelry, and once, allegedly, her date. Nothing had ever gone missing for good, though. Just borrowed... for weeks. Another long shot, but a lead nonetheless.

We walked into the kitchen and collided with a wall of noise from the backyard. Bathing suits, wet towels, music, and cocktails had taken over the patio. I was very much overdressed.

"Oh my god," a girl near the sliding door called out. "You must be cooking in those pants! I'm starting to get heat stroke just looking at you."

"She's working," Lucy said flatly, scanning the patio. "Have you seen Melody?"

The girl raised an eyebrow. "Did you find your missing makeup box? Are we done with that drama? We kind of miss you out here."

Lucy ignored the jab. "Melody!" she called.

A brunette in the pool glanced over, clearly unimpressed. She rolled her eyes and turned back to two guys splashing beside her.

"See what I mean?" Lucy muttered, storming outside.

I stayed by the kitchen entrance, choosing dry clothes and dignity over cannonball diplomacy. Bruno brushed against my leg, tail alert, eyes fixed on Lucy.

"What's her problem now?" a guy asked as he approached me.

"No clue," said another, a tattoo peeking from under his tank top. "Feel bad for Johnathan. He doesn't know what he's getting into."

The first guy nudged him with a warning glance in my direction.

"I mean, she's beautiful and smart," Tattoo Guy said quickly. "Just... a little bossy."

"Louis Cullens," the first guy said, extending a hand. "I don't think we've met."

"Margaret Willow," I said, shaking his hand. "Sandie's sister. You've likely met her already."

"Of course. She's been super sweet to all of us, which I'm sure is hard with a house full of chaos."

"She should take notes," I said lightly. "Not that far off from her future, after all."

Louis laughed, and Tattoo Guy finally cracked a smile.

"So tell me, Margaret Willow," Louis said, gesturing toward the pool, "are you joining the party?"

Before I could answer, voices from the pool spiked.

"I don't care what you want, Lucy," Melody shouted. "I'm here to have fun. If you didn't want that, don't invite me!"

Lucy screamed back, standing at the pool's edge like a scolding lifeguard.

She wouldn't jump in—I knew that much. Even though she learned to swim with Sandie and me as kids, a river incident in high school had left her terrified of deep water.

"That's enough," Tattoo Guy barked, storming up to her. "Relax."

Before I could intervene, he picked her up and tossed her into the pool.

I wasn't sure which happened first—Lucy hitting the water or Bruno launching himself after her like a torpedo.

"Who brought that dog?" someone yelled as I bolted to the poolside. Only Lucy remained in the water, splashing in sheer panic.

"Lucy!" I called. "Bruno's got you—grab on!"

Bruno swam straight to her, circling once before nudging his body beneath her arm. Slowly, carefully, he guided her toward the edge. I dropped to my knees, grabbed her wrists, and pulled her out. After that, we were both dripping wet.

"I didn't know she couldn't swim," Tattoo Guy said, guilt creeping into his voice.

A tall man with shaggy hair and a dropped drink came rushing from the patio. "What the hell is going on?"

He didn't wait for an answer. "Lucy!" he said, kneeling beside her.

"Johnathan," Lucy mumbled, her face hidden in his shoulder.

"What were you thinking, Theodore?" he shouted. "I've told you—your jokes are only funny to Granny!"

Bruno jumped out and gave me a full-body shower as he shook himself dry beside me.

"Well," Louis said, offering his hand, "that was a strange turn of events."

I accepted the towel he handed me and asked, "What do you mean by that?"

He bent to rub Bruno's ears. "Well, up to this morning, Theodore was Lucy's biggest family fan. And trust me, this isn't the first time we've chilled by a pool, and even *I* know Lucy is scared of water."

That caught my attention. "Any idea what happened?"

From the other side of the patio, Lucy waved frantically. "Maggie!"

"See?" Theodore muttered. "Bossy and unforgettable."

"It's her wedding week," Louis said.

"I don't think I could handle Lucy for more than a weekend," Theodore muttered as he sipped his neon cocktail.

Louis turned to me. "Sorry, Margaret, this is Theodore Cullens. Johnathan's younger brother."

I gave him a long look. "Not happy with her, huh?"

Theodore lifted his glass. "She has been... something."

"Maggie!" Lucy shouted, louder this time, which made them both laugh. The smirk on Theodore's face as he raised his glass was enough to make me sick.

I held my tongue, though, and walked toward Lucy. I'd need to talk to them again. Preferably when they were sober.

It didn't take long for Sandie to appear at the patio door, waving at me with urgency.

"I can stay with your dog," Louis said, grinning. "That way, I'll know you have to come back."

After years with Andrew, the flirtation caught me off guard. My awkward reply didn't help.

"Bruno doesn't stay with strangers unless he's arresting them. But I'm sure I'll see you around."

"Arresting me?" Louis stood, brushing water from his legs. "That explains it—he knew how to rescue Lucy. He's a police dog."

"A K-9," I corrected, Bruno rising to follow me without hesitation.

"I'll look forward to talking to you again, Margaret Willow," he called.

Unfortunately, my sister overheard him. The look she gave me said *we're going to talk about that later*, and the one I gave her said *please don't—at least not now*.

"Come on!" Sandie urged as soon as I stepped inside. "Lucy's going to kill her."

We followed the shouting echoing down the hall. The house was huge, but the layout was simple, and the yelling made it even easier to find our way. I stepped into what looked like a library or a large study—shelves lining the walls, dusty sunbeams pouring through the tall windows.

Melody stood near the fireplace, arms crossed defiantly. Lucy, red-faced and trembling, was being held back by Johnathan.

"You're just mad because I'm better than you!" Melody screamed.

"You're not better than anyone, Melody! You've always been jealous. That's why you took it! You *stole* it!"

Johnathan held Lucy close, his arms around her waist, but he struggled to maintain his grip.

Before I could warn Lucy about what she was revealing in front of him, Melody snapped back:

"Yeah, I took it! But I was going to give it back tonight. You're just overreacting. Like always."

"Where is it?" Lucy shouted, trying to break free again. "Give it back! It's a family heirloom! You have no idea what you—"

Melody faltered, frown deepening. "An heirloom? It's just some ridiculous makeup box."

Lucy stopped fighting. Her knees buckled, and if Johnathan hadn't caught her, she would've hit the floor. He held her as her body sank, his arms still tight around her.

Tears welled in Lucy's eyes, but Johnathan's face held something deeper than shock—worry and disbelief.

"Lucy..." His voice was quiet, shaky. "Did you lose my family's necklace?"

She didn't answer with words. Her tears did that for her.

Sandie rushed to her side, kneeling beside her and wrapping her arms around her. Bruno gave a soft whimper, pressing close to my leg, tail down, ears perked.

Melody's gaze flicked to him, and something in her expression shifted—regret, maybe, or just the weight of being seen.

"Whatever you lost, it wasn't me who took it," she said, her voice low now. "And I want nothing to do with this anymore."

She turned toward the door.

"You know, Lucy... I used to look up to you. I thought you saw me as family, like a sister. That's why I borrowed your stuff. And I always gave it back."

She paused, hand on the doorframe.

"I'll leave your makeup box on your bed. Good luck with your wedding."

She left without another word. Bruno

shifted beside me, ears twitching, but didn't move.

I let her go. Whether she was telling the truth or not, now wasn't the moment to dig deeper. She was furious. Lucy was falling apart. And Johnathan... he looked like he'd just watched a bridge crumble under his feet.

Bruno padded toward him, slow and tentative, then rested his head gently on Johnathan's knee. The gesture surprised me—and apparently Johnathan too. He reached down, absently stroking behind Bruno's ears as if the contact grounded him.

"I didn't know," he whispered, mostly to himself. "I thought it was just... just makeup."

"We're going to find it," I said, quietly but firmly.

Johnathan didn't respond. He kept his eyes on the floor.

Chapter 8

"I told Lucy we should call the police—" I began, but Johnathan cut me off with a frantic shake of his head.

"No. My mother can't know about this. She'll cancel the wedding, and then—who knows what she'll do."

Sandie let out a loud groan and shifted her weight like her heels were starting to turn into torture devices. She scowled at him. "You're a grown man, Johnathan. Your mother doesn't get to decide who you marry."

"She can't stop me," he muttered, pressing the heels of his hands to his eyes. "But she can send my fiancée to prison."

"I didn't steal it," Lucy said softly, her voice trembling. "I swear I didn't. I don't care about your family's wealth. I love you."

Johnathan reached out and clasped her hand, his voice gentler now. "You don't have to swear anything to me. I know you, Lucy. I love you, too. I won't let my mother hurt you. I'll tell her it was my fault—that I lost it. I'll take the blame."

"She won't believe that, and you know it," Lucy replied, looking exhausted. Then her eyes turned to me. "Would you still help us? Please, Maggie?"

Bruno, who had been lying at my feet, lifted his head at the sound of my name and gave a soft, huffing sigh—his way of saying *I'm listening too.* He padded closer and leaned against my leg, anchoring me to the moment.

I didn't have to think long. I couldn't stand the idea of Lucy behind bars. And if her future mother-in-law had her own son this terrified, then yes—she had to be someone very special. The dangerous kind of special.

"Of course I'll help," I said. "But our deal still stands. You need to come clean during the rehearsal."

Johnathan stood, running a hand through his hair. "She can't. My mom would—"

"And what's your plan?" I said, raising my voice just slightly. "Pretend the necklace didn't vanish before the wedding? Do you honestly think your mother won't notice a giant stone missing from Lucy's neck at the altar? Or will you give her your compass, hoping she'll accept it as the new family heirloom?"

He sat back down, this time settling closer to Lucy and entwining their fingers. Bruno padded forward and rested his chin on Lucy's knee with a quiet whine. She gave him a weak smile and rubbed behind his ears—probably the only comforting thing she'd done all day.

"You're right," Johnathan said at last. "But do you think you can actually find it? Or at least find out who took it? If I can give my mother someone to blame, maybe I can control the fallout."

That gave me a tiny shred of hope. If the necklace wasn't already melted down and pawned, maybe there was a chance. Finding the person might be simpler than recovering the item itself. *Might.*

"I'll give it a try," I said. "Lucy thought Melody couldn't have taken it, but maybe Louis?"

Johnathan's brow furrowed as he looked at Lucy.

"I thought you liked Louis."

"I do," she admitted. "But he always has an angle. He's smart enough to know how to sell the necklace and disappear... And honestly, I don't think he even likes me that much."

Johnathan didn't argue. He just kissed the back of her hand and held on tighter.

I glanced over at Sandie, who stood with arms crossed, her mouth pressed into a skeptical line. She didn't need to say anything. I could read it in her eyes: *this whole family is trouble.*

"What about Theodore?" I asked, curious.

They both frowned and shook their heads.

"I know he tossed me into the pool, but Theodore loves me," Lucy said—then quickly amended, "I mean, he likes me being part of the family."

Johnathan wasn't fazed. "I know what you meant, but Theo's harmless. He's always been the fun and easygoing one in the family. Granny's favorite and all. I'm sure he doesn't care about the heirloom."

Sandie let out a short, amused puff. "Well, if he *is* Granny's favorite, why would he?"

Lucy gave her a warning look, but Johnathan laughed.

"Granny's the oldest member of the family, but she already gave us our part of her estate. You're right, Sandie—he got a big chunk."

"So the family fortune... it's your mother's?" I asked slowly.

Johnathan nodded. "She's the one who controls everything now."

And just like that, the small sense of relief I'd been clinging to shriveled up. Of course, it was the matriarch. I had a bad feeling about this—like someone in the shadows was preparing an offer I wouldn't be allowed to refuse.

Bruno gave another low huff and walked to me. I reached down and scratched behind his ears.

"Looks like we're in deep again, boy," I whispered.

Bruno licked my hand and settled down next to me, watchful as ever.

Chapter 9

As I was driving back to the office, Linda called to let me know Martin Norton wanted to speak with me. I wasn't surprised. I had just shut down the most popular section of the country club, and I knew plenty of golfers weren't going to be thrilled. Still, as the city manager, Martin wasn't just my boss—he was Pat's too—and frankly, he should've handled Pat Potter's attitude problem a long time ago.

I hadn't expected to find Martin in the City Hall lobby, deep in conversation with Norman Beltran—our operations and maintenance manager, which probably meant the country club was involved—and Chief Ben Morales, who I hoped was there to offer support, not on official police business. Given the way things had been going lately, I half expected someone to tell me they'd found a body.

Bruno didn't hesitate. The second he spotted them, he bounded across the lobby and launched himself straight at Ben, tail wagging furiously. Ben staggered back a step as Bruno practically tackled him with a flurry of happy licks.

"Bruno!" Ben shouted, laughing despite himself as he tried to fend off the affection. "One day you're going to send me to the hospital, you big beast."

Despite his words, he crouched down and gave Bruno a solid scratch behind the ears. Bruno responded by thumping his tail on the tile floor like he owned the place.

"So, Bruno's working with Maggie now?" Martin asked as I joined them.

"I don't know," Ben said, ruffling the fur on Bruno's back. "Maybe this guy needs a vacation too."

The way they said it made my internal alarms start ringing. I glanced between them, trying to read their faces. Something wasn't right.

"Did something happen to Logan?" I asked, heart suddenly tight in my chest.

Ben let out a long groan and stood, his face clouding over. "Yes! Something happened. He decided to ignore direct orders. And to make my week even better, I had to suspend my medical examiner too."

Norman chuckled, and Martin shook his head with that familiar *I'll pretend this isn't chaos* expression. I was about to press for more details when Ben turned on me, jabbing a finger in my direction.

"Did you have something to do with this too? Where have you even been? And why aren't you in your office?"

I blinked, caught off guard. Before I could answer, Bruno stepped protectively between us and gave a single, soft woof—just enough to remind Ben whose side he was on. I scratched the back of Bruno's neck and faced Ben.

"I had an emergency at the golf course. That's where I've been. I'm not sure what you think I did."

Martin folded his arms. "She's right. There's a situation out there we need to handle —preferably before the golf association sues us."

Ben groaned and narrowed his eyes. "This sounds exactly like the kind of mess you'd get involved with, Margaret. Are you sure there's nothing you need to tell me?"

I tilted my head, honestly confused—until it hit me. "You're talking about the heist?"

Ben's scowl deepened, and he opened his mouth to respond, but I beat him to it.

"I had nothing to do with that, Ben. The only reason I know anything is because my mom mentioned it. Arthur said something this morning when I talked to Logan."

Ben didn't seem convinced, but Martin stepped in again. "I really don't think Margaret's involved in this one. She's been dealing with Potter—frankly, that's punishment enough."

Norman muffled a laugh behind his hand while Ben glared at Martin.

"No one can work with Potter," Ben muttered.

"Exactly!" Norman said, pointing for emphasis. "The guy's impossible. You know how many fights we've had just over landscaping? And now he wants us to wait till the end of fall to clean the golf course ponds? You know how tough it is to deal with frozen water? Martin, come on. Margaret's great, but she's not a miracle worker."

I wasn't exactly feeling reassured by any of this.

Martin ignored the protests. "I know he's difficult. But right now, the priority is finding someone with a strong personality—and experience—to manage the country club for the next couple of weeks."

"And where do you think we'll find this unicorn?" Norman asked, incredulous. "I helped cover the R-Parks department after Troy left, but this? This is not my world."

I turned to Ben, remembering his earlier frustration. "So what exactly did you do to Logan?"

Ben sighed and rubbed his temples. "Suspended him. Two weeks. He's lucky I didn't bench him for a month, or until a doctor clears him to come back."

I couldn't help it—I threw my arms around him in a sudden, impulsive hug.

Ben stiffened, and the three men stared at me like I'd lost my mind.

"I'm not sure Logan would appreciate your enthusiasm," Norman said dryly.

"You're right," I admitted, stepping back. "Do you know where he is?"

Norman scratched his chin. "Either at home... or at the tavern."

"I'll call you as soon as I wrap this up, Martin," I said, already heading toward the exit. The urgency in my chest was real now, and I didn't try to hide my grin. Bruno trotted at my heels, then jogged ahead to hold the door open with his nose—like the best assistant a sleuth could ask for.

I needed to talk to Logan.

Once I got into my car, I called Logan. After a brief three-minute conversation, I let him know I was on my way to his apartment—I needed to talk to him.

I found him sitting at one of the picnic tables outside his building. Well, Bruno found him first. My clever pup sniffed the air, caught Logan's scent, and trotted ahead. Instead of bounding toward him like usual, Bruno slowed and gently pressed himself against Logan's leg. It was the same gentle, comforting gesture he'd been doing since Logan got shot—like he knew his friend needed a softer kind of company now.

Logan smiled faintly and scratched behind

Bruno's ear before glancing up at me. He gave a half-shrug as I sat across from him.

"I assume you heard I got suspended?"

His shoulders drooped. That usual laid-back ease in his posture was gone, and a twinge of guilt hit my stomach. Norman's sarcastic jab from earlier echoed in my mind. Maybe I shouldn't have felt so lucky about the timing of this.

"What happened?" I asked. Then, guessing aloud, "Arthur messed up the investigation?"

Logan let out a long sigh and shook his head. "Arthur. He's the worst at keeping things under wraps. Apparently, you weren't the only one he ran into this morning. He told half the town about my plan to check in on the heist."

"You probably should've picked a better clandestine partner," I said, expecting a half-smile and sarcastic comeback.

Instead, Logan leaned forward and looked me straight in the eyes. "You mean I should've chosen you?"

The sunlight was conveniently bright enough to excuse the sudden warmth creeping into my cheeks. I cleared my throat and changed the subject before things drifted into emotionally dangerous territory. "Why were you so interested in the heist?"

"Who isn't?" Logan leaned back with a spark in his eyes. "This is history, Maggie. That necklace was worth millions, and the way it was taken? Brilliant. It's the kind of case they turn into documentaries. A once-in-a-lifetime puzzle."

I couldn't help but chuckle. "I didn't know you wanted to be a celebrity."

He smirked and reached down to pet Bruno, now curled at his feet like a guard dog on break. "Not a celebrity. I just wanted to solve it. You know the feeling, don't you?"

My mind flashed to the famous missing painting from the museum just a few weeks ago, and I smiled, looking away so he wouldn't see how much that hit home. "Yeah," I admitted softly. "I know the feeling."

"Ben said it's a fourteen-day suspension," I added. "You got any plans for your unexpected vacation?"

Logan raised an eyebrow. "Should I have plans for it?"

No more dodging. I felt a little guilty for using the opportunity, but I needed his help—and not just because he had a badge.

"I kind of need your expertise..."

He straightened. "I don't think Lucy's

going to want my help, Maggie. Whatever she lost—I'm sure you can find it."

I blinked. I didn't think he'd come to that conclusion. And the way he brushed it off... it irritated me.

"First of all, it's *also* a necklace," I said, annoyed. "An expensive family heirloom. And second, she didn't lose it. I'm sure someone took it."

Logan's sarcasm faded. "If you think it was stolen and it's that important, then you already know what you're supposed to do."

"And you did that?" I countered, narrowing my eyes. "Let the police handle it?"

"I *am* the police," he said, grinning wide.

"But you weren't assigned to the case," I pointed out. "That puts you in the same position as me. A private investigator."

Logan let out a breath. "I doubt Lucy wants me sniffing around, especially with my current *employment development.*"

"It's not a robbery," I corrected him with a smirk. "It's a theft. No one got hurt."

"Oh, so now you're a lawyer?" he teased. But then he asked, "How valuable is this necklace, anyway? You need a motive. The wicked mother-in-law isn't enough."

I hesitated. Honestly, I didn't know the

exact value. When I didn't answer, Logan raised an eyebrow.

"Basic info, Maggie. If you're going to track it down, you need to know why someone would take it."

"So now you're helping me?"

He lifted his good arm in a dramatic shrug. "Isn't that why you're here?"

I probably gave something away in my expression, because his face shifted again—more serious now.

"What kind of expertise are we talking about?"

I bit my lip, then practically mumbled, "Kitchen expertise? Did you hear about the country club?"

Bruno perked up at the word *kitchen*, tail thumping once against the table leg.

Logan raised an eyebrow. "You're dragging me into golf course politics now?"

"I need a partner with a strong personality, as Martin put it... and decent taste in sandwiches," I said with a wink.

Logan laughed, and even Bruno gave a huff, like he was in on the joke.

"What in the world?" Logan exclaimed after I finished explaining everything. "Maggie, I don't know how I can help you with this."

I sighed and looked down at Bruno, who had taken to resting his head on my foot under the table—his warm weight grounding me.

"Well," I started, brushing my hair behind my ear, "you ran Cyder's Pub for years... and you did look bored this morning, so I thought—"

"I haven't worked in a restaurant in a very long time, Maggie," he said. But when I met his gaze, his expression was more concerned than offended. I exhaled with relief. The last thing I wanted was to come off as insensitive, especially given his current situation. Norman was right —I wasn't exactly being delicate about it.

"It's just for a few days," I explained. "Martin and I are trying to find a permanent solution, but we can't keep the golf course open without food service. We'll lose players, and apparently, the golf associations are already upset."

Logan crossed his arms and gave me a pointed look. "And you think Larry O'Leary and Felix are going to keep things afloat?"

When I didn't answer, he chuckled and

shook his head. "You haven't even talked to them yet, have you?"

"Mr. Elliott said he'll loan Felix—if there's someone competent running the kitchen. And I know Mrs. O'Leary can convince Larry if she wants to. I just need someone who knows what they're doing to pull it together."

Logan smiled and leaned forward, resting his elbows on the table as Bruno nudged his knee, tail thumping once. "I appreciate the vote of confidence, I really do. But I don't want to disappoint you. Especially not at a golf course. Aren't those restaurants supposed to be... fancy?"

"Some of them, sure. But this one's city-owned. It's more of a casual hangout after the game than a white-tablecloth dinner spot."

He rubbed his face and frowned. "And will I have to deal with the wedding? Because if Lucy doesn't want my help with the... robbery —" He paused to smirk. "Sorry, *theft*—I can't imagine she'll want me catering for her wedding."

"You won't have anything to do with the catering," I assured him. "But... I'd honestly love having someone I trust keeping an eye on that family business."

That got his attention. His smile faded. "You think there's something off with them?"

"That's the thing," I said slowly, the words tightening in my throat. "I asked Terry if he'd heard from them since he ran the food for the art festival—nothing. Everyone knows everyone's business in this town. Sure, they say the business is based in Maple Hollow, but still... and what Mr. Elliott mentioned isn't good. It seems a little too convenient to me. Pat found this Nico the same day he fired our city caterer?"

Logan scratched behind Bruno's ears thoughtfully. Bruno leaned into it, making a soft huff of contentment.

"Do you even like this Pat guy?" he asked.

I laughed bitterly. "Pat is... complicated. As a golfer, he's great—or at least was. As a coach he was tough but fair. Helped us win championships. But as a person? He's arrogant. Always has to be right, gets his way, and loves putting others down."

Logan rested his arms on the table between us. "Has he been unhappy with the city lately? Maybe something changed that pushed him to act out?"

I opened my mouth to answer, but before I could, Logan's expression shifted. His smile widened, and there was a glint of curiosity in his eyes. "That's what *I* need to figure out."

I blinked. "*You* need to figure it out?"

"I'll help you with that too. Something tells me I'm going to be running into this guy more often than not."

I sat back, studying him. "Does this mean you'll help me run the restaurant?"

He tilted his head, tone suddenly warm. "Absolutely... or until you fire me because I mess up the whole golf course."

Without hesitation, I leaned across the table and hugged him. I was careful not to jostle his arm, and he hugged me back with the one that wasn't injured. It felt... right.

Until he opened his mouth again.

"So I'll see you tomorrow at 5 a.m.?"

I pulled back. "What?"

He grinned as he stood, brushing some dirt from Bruno's back. "Maggie, it's the food industry. You've got to start early if you want to get anything done."

Bruno stood and gave a soft bark of agreement—traitor.

"Five *a.m.*," Logan grumbled as he started walking toward his apartment.

"*Six-thirty,* and I'm the boss!" I called after him.

Logan turned around, walking backward with a grin. "Six *a.m.* or this whole thing's off!"

Bruno looked up at me, wagged his tail, then trotted after Logan like he'd already chosen his new kitchen team.

"Bruno," I shouted. "*You're* with me."

He turned, ears down and tail slow.

"Seriously, I'm the one trying to protect your beauty sleep."

Chapter 10
Thursday...

I walked into the country house with a large mug of coffee in hand and a frown on my face. Thank goodness it was a beautiful day and the sun was shining bright— my sunglasses did a decent job hiding how grumpy I felt.

Bruno padded beside me, nose twitching at every bush and flowerpot we passed. He seemed far more excited about the early morning than I was. His tail swished with a cheerful rhythm as we headed toward the restaurant entrance.

The sound of clattering pans and chairs being dragged echoed through the building. I figured Logan was already getting things ready —but then I heard muffled voices from up-stairs. They didn't sound friendly.

The country club had grand stairs in front for guests, but I was heading for the service staircase tucked beside the kitchen. Just as I turned into that hallway, the door flew open.

"This doesn't involve you!" a deep voice barked, sharp and commanding. I couldn't see who he was talking to—just the tail end of a heated exchange. The other man swore, then shouted back even louder: "But do something, and I'll make sure you regret your life!"

Before I could get a better look, the door started to swing shut.

And then a hand landed on my shoulder.

"What are you looking at?"

I jumped, nearly spilling my coffee. Bruno barked and stepped in front of me, hackles raised and ready to defend.

I muffled a scream with my hand, heart thudding so hard it echoed in my ears.

"Dear goodness, Logan!" I wheezed once I caught my breath.

He bit back a laugh, arms folded and far too pleased with himself. "That's what happens when you sneak around the hallways and show up late."

Bruno gave a soft growl and nudged my leg like he was confirming I was still in one piece. I bent down and gave him a quick scratch behind the ear.

"You're lucky I didn't throw this coffee at you."

He eyed my mug with genuine concern.

"And for the record, I'm not late. I said 6:00 a.m.," I added, pushing my sunglasses onto my head.

"Sure thing, boss," he replied, tone teasing. "Come on. Let me show you the progress we've made."

I took a step forward, but something about the earlier shouting held me in place. I looked back at the hallway, uneasy. Bruno had his nose in the air, sniffing toward the stairs.

Logan noticed and stepped beside me. "What is it?"

"There was a man yelling at someone upstairs," I said. "He sounded furious—and he threatened the other guy."

Logan huffed. "Yeah, I know. They've been going at it all morning."

"Who exactly?"

"I assume it's the caterer and his team. When I got here, three of them were already knee-deep in an argument."

I planted my hands on my hips and gave him a pointed look. Bruno mirrored me by sitting upright between us, like he was waiting for the verdict.

"Isn't that... suspicious?" I asked.

Logan shook his head, chuckling as he turned toward the kitchen. "Maggie, if I flagged every loud disagreement as suspicious, I'd never get anything done. People fight—especially under pressure."

Still, something about that threat didn't sit right with me.

Bruno didn't seem thrilled either—his ears stayed perked as we followed Logan into the kitchen. His tail wasn't wagging now. He stuck close to my side, glancing back at the stairs with a low, uneasy rumble.

I wasn't sure what it meant, but I decided I'd trust both my instincts—and Bruno's.

Whatever that shouting match was about, I had a feeling we hadn't heard the last of it.

The kitchen was in complete chaos—boxes of food, dining ware, and supplies scattered across the floor like someone had opened every shipment at once and walked away.

Bruno padded beside me, tail high, but

even he paused at the sight. He sniffed cautiously at a rolling can of chickpeas before nudging it back toward a corner like he was tidying up. Good boy.

By the sink, Larry O'Leary gave me a half-hearted wave—more defeated than cheerful. But when Felix emerged from the walk-in freezer carrying a box, he greeted me with a full, bright smile.

"Hi, Margaret—I mean, boss," he corrected quickly, shooting a look toward Logan.

"Morning, Felix. And Margaret is fine."

He shook his head as he set the box on a nearby counter. "Forest warned us to call you boss. And he's a police officer, so, you know—we follow orders."

Larry gave me a weary thumbs-up from behind a stack of pots. "Yes, boss."

I chuckled despite myself, then frowned when I realized Logan had vanished from the kitchen. Bruno tilted his head and trotted off through the swinging door that led to the dining room.

"Well," I said to the guys, "thank you both. You're lifesavers. Truly."

From beyond the swinging door, I heard Logan moving something heavy, followed by his voice calling out:

"Come on, Maggie. I need to show you something in here."

Bruno stood waiting at the door, nose pressed to the window, tail wagging like he'd been summoned too. I gave the kitchen crew a grateful smile and followed him through.

The dining room hit me like a gut punch.

Tables were stacked, chairs overturned, boxes everywhere, and a giant mound of mismatched linens in the center of the room like a cotton avalanche. It was a far cry from the polished, ready-to-open space I'd seen just yesterday.

Bruno let out a soft whine and began weaving through the clutter, sniffing each pile like he was trying to make sense of the mess.

"What happened in here?" I asked, heading toward Logan, who stood at the bar tapping buttons on the register.

He looked up, scanned the room, and shrugged like it was nothing unusual before turning back to the machine.

"We're doing inventory before opening," he said, sounding exactly like Darcy when she proudly reorganized a toy mess instead of cleaning it.

"You were right to shut it all down yesterday," he added, more seriously.

That caught my attention. "What makes you say that? I mean—thanks—but...?"

Logan frowned and set three heavy binders on the counter. "The cash flow in this place is a mess, Maggie. None of the records make sense. This register's history is jumbled, and the bookkeeping is all over the place. I mean, Cyder's Pub had its problems, but at least those two tried to hide them. Here? No effort at all."

I opened one of the binders. Spreadsheets, numbers, and scribbled notes swam before my eyes like ancient Greek.

"I can try to go through this, but I can't run the restaurant and untangle whatever this is."

I shook my head. "I'll ask Sophie to review everything. You're the only one who can get this place running."

Before he could respond, a voice exploded from the far side of the room.

"I'll be the one deciding who runs this place—or not!"

Pat Potter barreled through the maze of

chairs and boxes like a wrecking ball in golf cleats.

"This is already a disaster!"

Bruno froze, ears back, body stiff beside me. I placed a calming hand on his back as Logan's expression turned stone-cold.

I took a deep breath, summoning every ounce of patience the early morning had to offer.

"Pat, you know better than that. The city decides who runs the country club—including the restaurant."

Pat scoffed and waved at the chaos. "If this is a sign of what our food service will look like, it's already doomed. And I've already talked to Nico—he's willing to take this dump over."

I rubbed my temple, but Logan cut in before I could reply.

"I'd say your help is what turned it into a dump."

Pat's eyes narrowed. "And who's our savior?"

This wasn't how I wanted the introduction to go, but it was too late now.

"Pat Potter, meet Detective Logan Forest. He's stepping in while Martin and I decide who to hire to manage the club."

Pat raised an eyebrow, sarcasm dripping. "A

detective? What is this—are you accusing me of something, Margaret? Or did the police department open a restaurant division?"

Logan gave a dry, humorless laugh. "Could be both. Unless you've got something to confess? Because these binders don't exactly scream honesty."

To my surprise, Pat didn't take the bait. Instead, he smacked the counter and grinned.

"I knew it! See? I was right to fire that joke of a chef. How much have we been losing?"

I didn't answer—not because I agreed, but because I didn't actually know. The binders were a disaster, not a smoking gun. And Pat certainly didn't need more confidence.

Instead, I turned to Logan, keeping my voice calm and businesslike.

"What do you need from me to make sure we open today?"

Bruno sat beside me, tail tapping quietly on the tile floor, eyes darting between Logan and Pat. And I couldn't help thinking—we might all need a bit of his quiet judgment right now.

Chapter 11

Although I didn't enjoy early mornings, I had to admit there was something satisfying about how much you could get done before the rest of the world woke up. It had been a hectic morning, but by 9 a.m., the restaurant was officially open. With any luck, the early golfers could grab a drink or snack at the turn—or, for non-golfers, that's right at the end of the ninth hole, halfway through the round.

I settled into one of the outdoor tables, cradling a hot coffee in my hands, and took in the peaceful view of the course. The fresh-cut grass glistened in the sunlight, and the breeze carried the faint sound of distant chatter and a few scattered "Fore!" shouts. Memories came rushing back—weekend tournaments, long practice sessions, Pat teaching me how to read the green. I'd loved golf from the first time I tried it. It was competitive, sure, but mostly it was a battle to beat your last score—to beat yourself.

Bruno, surprisingly calm, sat beside me with his ears perked and his gaze fixed on the pond nestled between holes one and nine. I half expected him to chase after the first golf ball that flew by, but he just watched the water like he was on lifeguard duty.

"Moment of truth," Logan said as he approached with a plate and a mischievous grin. He set it down in front of me with the pride of someone serving a masterpiece. A perfectly poached egg rested on a slice of toasted bread, flanked by crispy bacon and tender asparagus.

I leaned closer and took a deep breath. The savory aroma reminded me I hadn't had breakfast. My stomach growled in agreement.

Logan handed me a fork and, just as I was about to dig in, he drizzled a creamy sauce over the top.

"Our chef told me to do this," he said with a smirk.

I raised an eyebrow. "Our chef?"

He didn't answer. Just motioned for me to take a bite. Bruno perked up at the sight of the food, sat up straighter, and began thumping his tail against my leg. I could practically feel him willing me to drop a piece.

The first bite was heaven. Salty, creamy, crispy perfection. I closed my eyes and sighed.

"This is amazing," I told Logan between bites. "Did you—?"

He laughed and sat down at the table. "Goodness, no. I didn't cook that. I can scramble eggs, but nothing this fancy. Remember, the tavern's food was all Mr. Elliot's doing."

I nodded and took another blissful bite. "So who made this? Felix?"

"You'd think so, but nope. Larry. Turns out Mrs. O'Leary passed on a whole arsenal of kitchen secrets."

I looked toward the kitchen and smiled. "Well, give my compliments to the chef. This is seriously impressive."

"Margaret Willow, what's so good? I might have to try it myself," said a voice from the path.

I looked up. A golfer stepped out of the sunlight, and once my eyes adjusted, I recognized Louis Cullens. He set his golf bag near the door, then strolled over and—of course—stopped to pet Bruno.

Bruno accepted the attention like a true professional, lifting his chin with pride.

"You're not supposed to pet him when he's wearing a vest," Logan said, trying for a stern tone but not quite pulling it off.

Louis pulled his hand back and raised his eyebrows. "Sorry! Won't happen again. No vest —got it." He slid into the empty chair across from me and smiled. "Louis Cullens," he added, extending his hand toward Logan.

Logan took a second longer than usual before accepting it. I noticed the flicker of caution in his eyes—he was usually warm with strangers, unless he saw them as potential suspects.

"Logan Forest," he said simply, skipping any mention of being a detective.

Louis turned his attention to my plate. "And this is what you were raving about. It does look good."

"It is," I said. "Are you finished golfing already? You must've started early."

He nodded toward his clubs. "I like to get out as much as possible. Lucy's schedule is... well, let's say it doesn't leave much room for leisure. Are you playing too?"

"Sadly, no," I said. "Just here for business today."

At my side, Logan stood and dusted off his hands.

"Better get back inside. Make sure the business part keeps running."

I glanced up at him. Something about his tone felt off, and he didn't meet my eyes as he walked away. Had I said something wrong? I didn't have time to figure it out—Louis was still watching him walk back toward the restaurant.

"Nice to meet you!" Louis called out, but Logan didn't acknowledge him. Just disappeared inside.

Louis looked back at me. "Did I say something? I didn't mean to interrupt. I'm sorry."

I shook my head. "No, you didn't. We've just had a long morning, and there's a bit of tension in the air. That's all."

"Is that why the restaurant was closed yesterday?"

"City drama," I said with a half-smile. "Like any big family."

Louis laughed. "Tell me about it."

I leaned forward, keeping my tone casual but curious. "Are you in a hurry? I've got to get back to work soon, but if you're free, I've got time for breakfast."

Bruno nudged my hand under the table as

if approving of the move—or maybe he was just hoping Louis would drop a piece of bacon.

Over the next half hour, I discovered two very surprising things:

Larry O'Leary was an amazing chef, and Louis Cullens' laugh was both genuine and contagious—something I hadn't expected, given Lucy's comments about the family.

Bruno lounged at my feet, tail gently thudding against the floor every time someone walked by with food. Occasionally, he'd glance up at Louis like he was still deciding whether to approve of the man. So far, the jury was out.

"So, you're telling me your aunt is evil?" I asked after Louis finished a story involving a gallon of milk, two mischievous boys, and a very creative punishment.

He wiped his mouth and grinned. "I wouldn't say evil... authoritarian and a little sadistic, maybe. She really took her role as head of the family to heart. I think she enjoys it a little too much."

This was my chance to dig a little deeper.

"What about your grandmother?" I asked,

keeping my tone light. "I thought the oldest member of the family usually took that role."

Louis tilted his head, lips pursed as if weighing how much to say. When he finally spoke, his voice shifted slightly—there was a trace of regret in it. Or maybe something else I couldn't quite place.

"I love Granny, don't get me wrong. But she has... a strong character." He chuckled and shook his head. "Honestly, it's a bit hypocritical for my aunt to be so hard on Lucy. She was in the same position once—marrying into the family without the 'right' background."

I leaned in slightly, feigning curiosity. "Because she was a few years older?"

Louis chuckled again and mirrored my posture, lowering his voice. "According to my mom, it was a huge scandal. Aunt Dorothy's family didn't bring any financial benefit, but Uncle Frederick married her anyway."

"That must've been tough," I said sincerely. "Hopefully things got better over time?"

Louis shook his head. "Not really. When my uncle got sick, he stepped away from the business and handed it all over to my aunt. She's been in charge ever since."

"That couldn't have been easy either."

"I was twelve, and I remember the fights at

Granny's house. Epic ones," he said, gazing upward with a strange smile—half nostalgic, half calculating. "Eventually, Granny pulled her fortune out of the business completely."

It sounded more like a family soap opera than real life.

Bruno let out a low huff beneath the table, as if he agreed.

Louis leaned forward again, voice softening.

"You know what's the saddest part?" he asked. The joy drained from his face. "My uncle died about five years ago. Since Granny's health declined, Aunt Dorothy became her legal guardian and has been taking care of her ever since. But... let's just say Granny wasn't thrilled."

I frowned, guessing out loud. "Is that why she gave her inheritance while she was still alive?"

Louis nodded, his jaw tightening. "It was a mistake. Granny used the original will, thinking the bulk of Uncle Frederick's share would go to my mom—but that's not how it worked. Instead, his part ended up with his wife, Aunt Dorothy. The second biggest went to Theodore. The rest of us got... reasonable portions."

"Reasonable?" I raised an eyebrow. "You're not mad about that?"

His cheerful expression returned like a light switch, and he sat back.

"Not really. My mom and Uncle Frederick built the business together. That's where the real legacy is. I actually donated my portion back to Granny. She needed it for housing and medical bills."

Bruno, still watching Louis closely, stood and stretched before resting his head on my knee—almost like he was asking, *Do we trust this guy?* I gently scratched behind his ears but didn't take my eyes off Louis.

"That's very generous of you," I said.

Louis leaned in again, more serious this time. "Please don't tell anyone about that. Granny's proud. She wouldn't want anyone thinking she needed help."

"Of course," I replied. "Your secret's safe."

He offered a soft sigh. "I just followed my aunt's example. Like I said, she's not evil... she just really likes being in charge."

Bruno gave another low huff and shifted closer to me, brushing Louis's leg with his tail. Louis didn't seem to notice—or maybe he just ignored it.

And despite his charm, something about

Montie Red

Louis Cullens—his polished delivery, the way his eyes stayed just a little too bright—made me think that if someone in this family had a secret worth hiding...

It might just be him.

Chapter 12

As soon as I finished breakfast, I walked back into the restaurant to check on how things were going with Logan. I was happy to see several tables already occupied and—much to my surprise—a couple of waitresses weaving between them, not looking too frazzled for our first day.

Bruno trotted confidently at my side, pausing now and then to sniff a dropped crumb or two. He gave a little tail wag each time someone smiled at him, which, let's be honest, was almost everyone.

I spotted Logan by the cashier, typing something into the register, and started walking toward him when someone called out from the main entrance.

"I'm so glad you're still here," Nicholas

Henson said, hurrying across the floor with a large binder, a stack of napkins in different shades of cream, and two small vases clutched awkwardly in his hands. "I could really use your help, Margaret."

Bruno moved protectively in front of me at first, sniffing Nico's shoes as if to assess his worth. I gave his leash a gentle tug, and he stepped back but kept his eyes locked on the man.

"Nico, how can I help you?" I asked, already sensing drama approaching.

He took a deep breath and gave me a weary smile. "The wedding events this week—the bride says she's a friend of yours?"

The second I nodded, his shoulders relaxed, and he looked genuinely relieved.

"Can you come with me? She's here, and… she's not very happy."

The last thing I wanted was to get caught in wedding drama. The missing necklace already had me on edge. But this was my chance to check in on Nico's work. And, after all, it was the city's fault—Pat's, to be exact—that Lucy's original caterer had been booted.

Bruno and I followed Nico upstairs to one of the rooms set aside for the wedding party.

Even from the hallway, I could hear the stomping and scattered complaints.

"We can always have the dinner at the house," came Lucy's familiar voice through the door, sounding exasperated.

"Maggie!" she gasped as soon as she spotted me. "This is a nightmare! This guy has no idea what's going on. I want my caterer back!"

Beside me, Bruno sat attentively, watching Lucy pace like a tennis match, his ears flicking with every raised voice.

I heard Nico sigh quietly next to me, clearly trying not to show frustration. I didn't know him well, and yes, I had my doubts—but I did know Lucy.

"What exactly is the nightmare?" I asked, keeping my tone level.

Lucy flung her arms up like a stage actress and marched across the room. "Everything!"

I gave her one of my mom's classic *pull-it-together* looks.

She let out a huff, then snatched a piece of fabric from the table. "To start with—this tablecloth! It's creamy white, not off-white like I requested last fall."

I turned to Nico. "Did the previous caterer take our supplies?" I wasn't an expert on linen, but after combing through the country club's budget for weeks, I did know how much we paid for dry cleaning them.

Nico shook his head. "I don't think so. The supply closets were full when Pat unlocked them."

"That's not possible, Maggie," Lucy said, clutching the cloth like it was a piece of evidence. "These aren't the ones I approved."

I took a calming breath. "Lucy, I'm positive these are the only tablecloths the country club owns. And more importantly, this won't ruin your wedding."

Bruno gave a quiet woof, almost like a supportive sigh, and rested his head against my leg.

Lucy groaned and paced a bit more before pointing accusingly at Nico. "He's changing the entire menu!"

At that, I truly sympathized with Nico. I'd been on the receiving end of Lucy's bridal wrath more than once. I turned to him calmly.

"Not the entire menu," Nico said, hands raised slightly in defense. "Just tonight's. There wasn't time to get fresh seafood for the paella, so we're preparing a Mediterranean dinner this evening and moving the paella to tomorrow's rehearsal dinner."

From the side, Sandie chimed in supportively. "I think that sounds good."

Lucy flopped into a chair with a dramatic sigh. "Fine! But I'm not paying anything extra for this catastrophe."

I wanted to teach her what an *actual* catastrophe looked like—but at least she was agreeing to something.

"Any other issues with Nico?" I asked.

Lucy gave him a dramatic once-over, then shook her head. I smiled—relieved—and subtly turned my back to her.

"Just go," I whispered to Nico.

He gave the quickest nod I've ever seen and disappeared from the room like he'd trained for it.

I was just about to follow when Lucy stopped me.

"There's another issue, Maggie."

I sighed. "I haven't forgotten about the necklace. I'm still working on it."

Sandie gave me an apologetic smile and turned toward the window. Something in my stomach twisted.

"Melody's gone," Lucy said, like she expected me to be shocked. Strange, considering she'd kicked Melody out of the wedding party in front of everyone the day before. "I can't have a groomsman walking alone, and Johnathan won't drop one of his friends from the party."

I froze. Please no.

"I need you to be my last bridesmaid," Lucy stated. "We dropped off Melody's dress at Mom's. I'm sure it'll fit you."

I opened my mouth, but before I could speak, Sandie's wide-eyed panic and desperate head shake shut me up fast.

"The gathering starts at 6 p.m. here," Lucy added. "Be on time. At least the restaurant is running again. Louis texted me that the food was *acceptable*."

Bruno gave a sharp snort at that, as if he, too, took offense at *acceptable*.

Lucy swept past me without waiting for my response, and Sandie mouthed *sorry* and *thank you* before trailing after her.

As the door shut, I stared at it for a moment. Bruno pressed close to my leg like he could feel the emotional whiplash. All I could think about was Logan—and how I was going to enjoy Lucy's reaction when she figured out he was the one running the country club.

I wanted to hug my desk when I finally arrived back at my office. It had been a wild morning—and it was barely 11 a.m. Bruno trotted in behind me, tail swishing lazily, like even he was ready for a nap.

Linda followed close behind, a stack of folders in her arms. Since the restaurant had reopened, she didn't seem to mind that I was running late.

"Just a few papers for you," she said, setting them down. "And Sophie helped put together a list of possible candidates to manage the restaurant. Unless, of course, Logan is changing careers."

I laughed, and a little of the tension finally eased from my shoulders.

"It was a brilliant idea," Linda added as I started signing the forms. "Did you get him in trouble?"

"No! If anyone stirred things up, it must've been Bruno."

At the sound of his name, Bruno perked up, ears twitching as he sat beside my chair like the perfect office assistant.

Linda, of course, kneeled to rub behind his ears. "This cutie? Never."

"Maybe if food is involved..." I said with a

smile as Bruno panted happily, clearly enjoying the attention.

"Is Sophie around?"

"She's working with Bert this morning," Linda said, scooping the remaining papers into a folder.

"Thanks."

I wasn't surprised to find Bert perched on the edge of a desk mid-monologue, while Sophie's eyes were locked on her screen, fingers tapping out a rhythm fast enough to rival a piano concerto.

"Margaret!" Bert shouted when he spotted me. He leaped off the desk like a game show host announcing a prize. "What brings you to this fine corner of this government's office on such a beautiful morning?"

Sophie paused typing just long enough to glance up.

"She's looking for me, Bert."

"How do you know that?" he asked, arms crossing.

"The binders under her arm." Sophie extended her hand toward me. "That looks like an accounting problem."

I handed her the binders. She was right.

Bert groaned dramatically, tossing his arms

into the air. "Smarty-pants." He turned to walk off, but I stopped him.

"Actually, I still need your help, Bert."

He spun around with a grin. "See, Sophie? She *is* here for me."

Sophie rolled her eyes and dove into the paperwork while I turned to Bert.

"What do you know about the country club?"

He ran a hand through his messy hair and gave a thoughtful huff. "Not much. We handle general maintenance. The last big renovation wrapped a couple of years ago. But that place has been in the red for a while."

That didn't explain why Pat was so upset with the caterer.

"What about the golf course?" I asked. "Any clues there?"

Bert scratched his chin. "Let me think. Last year, we installed a new irrigation system—all paid out of the course's profit. This year, there's a landscaping service, an exterior wash, and the pond cleaning on the schedule."

"An exterior wash? Shouldn't that be budgeted under the country club?"

"It should, but the contract says any annual over-budget maintenance falls into the golf course's budget."

I raised an eyebrow. "So, the course has been paying for the club's expenses for years?"

"Exactly. And Pat's not thrilled. Every time he pays for the building, that money isn't going back into the course."

Behind her screen, Sophie muttered almost too quietly to hear, "This might be part of it..."

I leaned forward. "What is it?"

Her cheeks flushed, but her voice grew steadier. "I need to double-check everything, but it looks like the books have been misreporting the restaurant and the catering as one single business."

Bert furrowed his brow. "Wouldn't that inflate their profits?"

Sophie shook her head. "Not in this case. The restaurant runs poorly during the off-season, but the catering side actually makes a steady income. Combining them might make the whole thing look unprofitable."

Suddenly, it all started making sense.

"Pat's clever," I said slowly. "He must've figured the caterer was hiding income by folding it into the restaurant's losses. And the caterer probably didn't mind, since it meant less responsibility for maintaining the building."

I turned to Sophie. "Let me know once

you've verified everything. If we're right, I finally have leverage with Pat. If he wants to protect the golf course budget, he'll have to let me hire a separate food service."

Bruno gave a low woof of approval, as if backing me up.

"Thanks, Bert!" I called as I turned to go, practically bouncing with energy. This wasn't just a break—it was a wedge I could use to get control back.

I'd barely reached the hallway when Terry stepped out of the elevator, waving a stack of papers.

"Margaret!" he called. "Don't go anywhere. I need to show you something!"

Bruno barked once and stepped in front of me, like he was ready to take on whatever "something" came next.

Terry rested his hands on his knees, bent over and catching his breath as soon as we walked into my office. I gave him a moment, but Bruno had other plans. Tail wagging like a metronome, he trotted over and enthusiastically licked Terry's hands—then went straight for his face.

"Bruno!" I called out, but of course, he ignored me completely.

"Hi, pal," Terry said, chuckling as he rubbed Bruno's head in thanks—or maybe just trying to get the dog to settle so he could catch his own breath. "I'm all right, buddy."

He plopped into the chair in front of my desk, and Bruno immediately settled by his feet like they'd been best friends for years. Terry kept one hand absentmindedly stroking behind Bruno's ears, which only made my dog melt into the moment.

I just hoped Logan didn't walk in right then and get huffy about Bruno *being on the clock.*

"I think I figured something out," Terry said, placing a stack of papers on my desk. "Took me a while, but it turns out our new friend Nicholas Henson *does* own a company —but it's not a catering one."

The weight that had just begun to lift from my shoulders came crashing back down, twisting into a knot in my stomach.

"He's not a caterer?" I asked slowly.

Terry shrugged. "Maybe... kind of? His

original company was an event business based in Maple Hollow."

"Event planning has to include catering," I said hopefully. I wanted to believe that. But Terry gently popped that balloon.

"Not the kind of events you're thinking of. They organized sports events—hockey tournaments, figure skating competitions, swim meets. From what I could gather, they mostly did video, photography, and scheduled vendors. Maybe food stands, but nothing close to running a full-service kitchen."

The temperature in the room felt like it dropped five degrees. I rubbed my eyes, already imagining Lucy's reaction when she found out her new caterer's expertise might be limited to reheating hot dogs and keeping a popcorn machine running.

"It's not all bad," Terry said, leaning in. "The Henson family closed that company last year. Nicholas got a catering license six months ago."

I didn't want to ask. I braced myself.

"That said," Terry continued, "I couldn't find any references to his services. No reviews, no website. His most recent tax report? Zero income."

"You got his taxes?" I blinked at him.

Terry sat up proudly, a broad grin on his face. "You asked me to dig. I dug."

I leaned back in my chair, eyes fixed on the ceiling tiles. "So... we're his first client?"

"Maybe," Terry replied. He shifted forward again, his tone dropping slightly. "This is just a rumor—I couldn't confirm it—but a friend in Maple Hollow told me that after the Henson company closed, Nicholas moved to the city and started doing fancy birthday parties. Like luxury ones, in upscale venues. Word is, he was networking hard."

I sighed. The facts weren't ideal, but I had to admit—Terry had done great work.

"Awesome job, Terry," I said sincerely, even if the news left me with more questions than answers. "Keep an eye on him. Let me know if you learn anything else."

Bruno let out a soft chuff and stood up as if he knew it was time for me to move again.

I looked down at him, then back at the file on my desk.

It was time to have another talk with Nico.

Chapter 13

Logan was chatting with a group of golfers by the bar when I stepped back into the restaurant—again. Considering I'd only eaten at the country club once in the past five years, this being my second visit today felt surreal.

"You just missed them," Logan said as he wrapped up with the group.

"Who?" I asked, making my way to the quieter side of the bar. It made me feel good to see the place bustling, especially after how it looked earlier—stacked with boxes, teetering on closure.

"Darcy and your mom."

I turned toward the entrance instinctively. "When? Why? I can't believe I missed my little girl."

"She's a keeper," Logan said, lifting his arm to show me a fresh scribble drawn in black permanent marker.

I squinted. A flower? A smiley face? Both, maybe.

"Logan!" I groaned. "I told her not to draw on your sling—it's not a cast!"

"Yeah, but I don't have a cast, and I couldn't disappoint her. You should've seen her face."

I sighed, but smiled as he poured me a glass of water and slid it across the bar.

"Did they eat?"

"Of course," he said, then lowered his voice, leaning in. "Although I feared for my life when your mom realized we didn't have seafood chowder."

I chuckled. That sounded about right.

"Is the day going okay?" I asked, though the answer seemed obvious from the energy around us.

Logan raised an eyebrow and put his good hand on his hip.

"Do you have to ask?"

I raised both hands in surrender. "Absolutely not. This was my idea, after all." Before he could reply, I got down to business. "Have you seen Nico? I have some questions for him."

His expression shifted instantly, closing like a door. He shook his head.

"If you need to talk to him, I'd rather be with you when you do it, if that's okay?"

He asked, but his tone didn't leave much room for a "no." That only made me more curious.

"Sure, but why?"

Instead of answering, Logan leaned across the counter and gave Bruno a scratch behind the ears. Bruno, who had just trotted in from the office hallway, wagged happily and leaned into the affection.

"You might want to use the opportunity and talk to that woman over there, though," Logan said casually.

I followed his gaze to a table by the far window. A woman sat alone, dressed in a sleek, light-gray suit that looked far above my city paycheck. She read a hardcover book, completely at ease—as if she didn't already command the room with her presence.

"Who is that?"

"Dorothy Cullens," he said.

I blinked. "When did she get here? What is she doing here? Does Lucy know?"

Logan tapped my hand with a sly smile. "Two of those are questions for her. As for

Lucy? I doubt she knows—but that's just a guess."

I frowned, but he held up a finger before I could say anything.

"You want to find that necklace?" he asked. "Figure out why it matters so much. Then you'll know whether you're dealing with a dear family heirloom... or if you need to talk to pawn shops around here."

He winked, then turned to greet a couple who had just walked in.

Pawn shops. Of course. Why hadn't I thought of that?

Luckily, Logan couldn't stop being one. *(Optional: "one" might be clearer as "a detective" or "a sleuth" if you want to clarify the punchline.)*

At my side, Bruno gave a small whine and nudged my hand, like he could sense I was hesitating.

"All right, partner," I whispered. "Let's go meet the matriarch."

Taking a deep breath, I started walking toward Dorothy Cullens' table, still unsure exactly what I'd say—but trusting something would come out.

Dorothy Cullens looked exactly how you'd imagine the matriarch of a wealthy family. From her perfectly upright posture and tailored gray suit to the quiet command in her eyes, everything about her whispered control and old money. Even the restaurant's teacup in her hand looked expensive.

"Mrs. Cullens," I said.

Instead of appearing annoyed at being interrupted during her afternoon tea, she set down her book and reading glasses with the kind of grace you see in historical dramas. She looked up at me with mild curiosity.

"You must be the maid of honor's sister," she said. Her voice was composed, her tone cool but not unkind. She motioned to the chair across from her. "Please, sit. I'm very fond of Sandie. I can't imagine doing anything but lying down when I was that far along in my pregnancies."

I smiled with genuine pride. "She's amazing. During my last few weeks, the only thing I wanted to do was eat ice cream and nap."

Dorothy gave a faint smile in return, then tilted her head. "It's my understanding your sister and Lucy have been friends since childhood?"

"They were classmates all the way through school," I said, settling into the chair.

She lifted her delicate cup. "Would you like something to drink? I'm rather curious about how you ended up joining the bridal party at such a late hour."

The question wasn't really a question. Before I could answer, she signaled for a waitress with a flick of her manicured fingers.

"I'm still wondering that myself," I muttered with a wry smile.

The waitress approached—young, maybe a high schooler working a summer job—and clearly nervous. Her eyes flicked to Dorothy, and her hands fidgeted with the notepad.

"Is everything all right, ma'am? I can take the tea back again or—"

Dorothy interrupted smoothly, her voice polite but with a distinct chill beneath the surface. "That won't be necessary. This will have to do for now. But Mrs. Willow here will need something to drink."

I smiled to ease the tension and ordered an iced tea. The girl nodded quickly and almost sprinted back to the kitchen.

At my feet, Bruno flopped down with a

thud, clearly unimpressed by Dorothy's manners. He gave a soft huff and rested his head on his paws, though I noticed his ears remained alert.

Dorothy glanced at him with a lifted brow. "He's very well-behaved."

"He's on duty," I said. "But I think even he's picked up on how formal this conversation is."

Dorothy smirked slightly, then took a sip of her tea.

"So tell me, Margaret. How did you get roped into this wedding party?"

I cleared my throat, easing into what I really needed to ask. "Well, I wasn't exactly asked. More like... informed. But you know how it is —once the bridal train gets rolling, you either jump aboard or get run over."

Dorothy chuckled, holding her cup elegantly between two fingers. "Tell me about it."

It was the first moment she seemed remotely human—exasperated, even. And just like that, I saw my opening.

"Has this been too hectic?" I asked, and by her expression, I knew she was ready to talk.

Chapter 14

I walked back to the bar after Mrs. Cullens left, feeling more concerned than I had before our chat. Apparently, Logan noticed something in my face, because he handed the waitress he'd been working with a small notepad and walked over to me.

"What is it?" he asked.

I hesitated, trying to gather my thoughts, but when I couldn't make sense of them quickly enough, I just shook my head. "I just have a terrible feeling about all of this."

Logan leaned an elbow on the counter, watching me carefully. "I'm taking a break in twenty minutes. Where do you want to talk— here or your office?"

I smiled, feeling the tiniest bit of relief. "Outside? Maybe in front of the club?"

He slapped the counter lightly. "I'll meet you there."

The day was bright but not hot—the kind of perfect summer afternoon that begged for golf or a long walk. I stepped outside and found myself wandering toward the driving range, past clusters of golfers and the soothing *thwack* of clubs hitting balls. It had been ages since I last played, but the open space and rhythm of the course stirred something nostalgic in me.

I stopped at the pro shop and borrowed a set of beginner clubs—ones the coaches used to lure in curious newcomers. Smart strategy: people took one lesson, hit a few balls, and boom—hooked. Golf was funny that way. Addictive.

By the time Logan joined me at the range, I had already swung at a couple of balls and mostly embarrassed myself.

"I kinda forgot you used to play," he said with a smirk, as another ball sliced off to the right.

"Lucky you remembered. Otherwise, you'd be asking me to play with you."

"Oh, I never play with people I can't beat," he joked. "And I hate losing."

I laughed, but the tension crept back in like

fog. I nudged a ball into position with my club and started talking.

"Mrs. Cullens... she had no problem bragging about her family's wealth, their travels, the wedding budget. But the moment I asked about the necklace, she shut down. Brushed it off like it didn't matter."

Logan frowned slightly, arms crossing as he watched me line up a shot.

"What do you mean?"

I hit the ball—not my best, but not awful—and let out a slow breath. "She made it sound like the necklace was nothing. A silly family tradition she didn't even like. Said it had no financial value, and even admitted she hated wearing it at her own wedding."

"Then why threaten to cancel the whole thing over it?" Logan asked, his tone sharp. "And why would someone steal it if it was worthless?"

"Exactly." I glanced down at Bruno, who had flopped in the grass a few feet away, rolling on his back and batting at a fluttering leaf. He looked blissfully unconcerned, which only made the knot in my stomach feel heavier.

"And get this," I continued, lowering my voice. "She told me the necklace came from her husband's family. Said her mother-in-law's mother found it in the woods while they were escaping Poland during the war."

Logan's eyebrows rose, just slightly.

"She said they were forced out of their home. That they didn't get out safely until Russia joined the Allies. It made me wonder... what if the necklace belonged to someone else? A family that didn't survive? Lucy thinks it's valuable. She's not exactly a jewelry appraiser—but she knows gemstones. Something feels off."

"Does Lucy have a picture of it?" Logan asked, the investigator in him fully activated now. "I might know someone who can check if it's in any of the World War II art and heirloom registries."

I blinked. "Dana?"

He held up his hands. "She lives in the art world. And she owes me a favor."

My last shot went farther, though it veered wildly off course—probably symbolic of how I felt. I sighed, picked up the empty basket, and slung the borrowed bag over my shoulder.

"Sandie left one in my office yesterday. I can grab it from my car and—"

"That won't work," Logan said. "I need a digital one. No city trips for me anytime soon."

His smile mitigated some of the annoyance I felt whenever he spoke of his ex-wife.

"I need to get back to the office."

"And I should get back to pretending I know how to run a restaurant," Logan said, falling into step beside me. Bruno trotted between us, his tail wagging lazily.

"Oh boy!" I blurted, causing both Bruno and Logan to stop in their tracks.

"What is it?" Logan asked, tensing.

"Sorry—nothing urgent. I just forgot to tell you what Terry found out about Nico."

Logan sighed and resumed our slow pace. "Terry. He really should've been a journalist. What did he dig up this time?"

I smiled—he wasn't wrong. Terry had a knack for research that rivaled any seasoned reporter.

"Turns out Nico's so-called catering business in Maple Hollow wasn't a catering business at all. It was an event planning company—and not even for parties. Sports events mostly."

"Was?" Logan asked, frowning.

"Yep. That company's been shut down for a while. But here's the kicker—Terry found out Nico registered a catering business here in the city about six months ago. No website, no clients, and his tax filings say he made zero income."

Logan's expression darkened, his jaw tight-

ening as he processed the information. He nodded, eyes narrowing in thought.

We kept walking, but the silence between
us felt heavier now—thick with unspoken
questions and growing tension. Mrs. Cullens
was hiding something, that much was obvious.
And now, with Nico's sketchy background and
his mysterious connection to Pat, everything
about this wedding felt more dangerous than
celebratory.

Even Bruno slowed his steps, ears flicking
as if he sensed the shift too.

Logan walked with me to return the golf bag
—though I suspected the real reason was to
sneak out through the side door and avoid
Sandie and, more importantly, Lucy. He
laughed when I told him how I'd accidentally
become part of the wedding party, and he
didn't believe me for a second when I claimed
it was the perfect cover to investigate the
missing necklace.

He was right, of course.

"Just let me get this straight," Logan said,
amusement still in his voice. "The wedding is

Saturday. The rehearsal's tomorrow—Friday. And today is...?"

I shrugged, giving a helpless shake of my head. "Not totally sure. I think Lucy wants a pre-wedding party dinner. A chance to wrangle everyone and remind them how serious this entire event is."

"That sounds like Lucy," he muttered. Then his steps slowed, his tone softening. "I don't remember my wedding being such a big deal."

I raised a brow, walking slower to match him. "Well, Dana and Lucy are very different women."

He nodded, then stopped completely. "How was your wedding?... I mean, since we didn't exactly exchange invitations."

I stared at the hallway wallpaper as if it had suddenly become the most fascinating pattern on earth. I didn't mind the question—it just hit harder than I expected. His asking meant he didn't know. And somehow, I didn't like that gap in our friendship.

"There was no wedding."

Logan's brow furrowed, and before he could ask, I added, "I never married Andrew."

He froze, his expression unreadable. For

years, I'd heard comments from my mom, friends, even strangers with opinions on my marital status. I never cared. But now, standing in a quiet hallway with Logan, his silence felt personal —like something vulnerable had cracked open.

I turned and started to walk. Bruno nudged my leg with his nose, sensing my unease, and walked alongside me. Loyal and silent.

"Why didn't you accept his proposal?" Logan asked.

I stopped, caught off guard. "What makes you think he proposed?"

Logan stepped closer, and for once, his smirk wasn't teasing—it was gentle. Almost reverent.

"Because he was smart enough to stay with you for five years. Why wouldn't he want to keep you forever? I know I would."

Heat rose to my cheeks. I looked down, pretending to adjust Bruno's vest, but he was watching me too, tail flicking once in quiet approval.

"We were good friends," I said. "Comfortable, really. But I always knew I wasn't his priority—and he wasn't mine. When I found out I was pregnant, I knew marrying him for that reason alone would've been the worst thing I could do."

Logan didn't say anything, but his gaze didn't leave me.

I exhaled and met his eyes. "I didn't want Darcy growing up thinking she was the reason we stayed together. If things worked out, I wanted it to be because they were right. If they failed, I didn't want her blaming herself. She deserves better than that weight."

Logan's expression softened into something deeper—respect, maybe. Understanding.

"That sounds just like you," he said quietly.

There was a stillness then. He stepped in—closer than before. My heart fluttered, and even Bruno rose to his feet, ears perked, sensing the shift in energy.

And then—a loud crash echoed at the end of the hallway, followed by a sharp scream.

Bruno barked once, low and alert, already moving toward the sound.

Logan's whole body tensed. "Stay here," he said, but I was already following him—Bruno beside me, every step full of tension.

Chapter 15

"I found it like this!" the young waitress from the restaurant said when Logan and I turned the corner.

On the floor, lying face down, was a man in a white shirt and black pants. My mind scrambled to understand how this could be happening again, while my body froze in place.

I watched Logan spring into action, dropping to his knees to check the man's neck, then his wrist. Before I could process what was happening, I heard his voice call out.

"Maggie, he needs a doctor. Call an ambulance."

That's when I realized who the man was—Nico, now on his back, face pale. His chest still moved up and down, shallow but steady. A bruise marked his forehead, probably from the fall. I couldn't tell if he'd collapsed in the hallway or fallen down the stairs—the door behind him was still ajar.

"Maggie!" Logan shouted.

I snapped out of my daze and grabbed my phone. As I dialed 911, my eyes scanned the hallway. Logan was kneeling beside Nico. There was no blood, no obvious injuries—just the girl, standing at the far end of the corridor, her hands covering her mouth in shock.

"What's your emergency?" a voice said through the receiver. While I explained the situation, something caught my eye—a wall-mounted phone a few feet away and a piece of paper on the floor beneath it.

I was about to reach for them when a voice echoed from above.

"What in the world?"

A very tall man with dark hair and a mustache stepped out of the stairwell and rushed toward Nico.

"Oh no! Nico! What happened?"

Logan didn't move from his position, but his eyes flicked up at the newcomer. "Do you know him?"

The man nodded and bent down as if to touch Nico, then hesitated and backed off, leaning against the wall. "He's my brother. We were just talking about the— Is he alive?"

His tone sounded concerned, but his wording struck me as strange. Most people would ask if someone would be okay— not *if* they were alive. Logan gave me a look that told me he didn't like the guy. Not sure why, I instinctively took a small step back and used my foot to nudge the phone farther away. Then I bent down and picked up the paper.

"What's that?" Nico's brother asked, his voice sharp. His gaze landed on the paper in my hand, and something about the way he stared at it made my skin crawl—cold, intense, and without a hint of kindness.

"I don't know," I said, and handed it to Logan.

The man stepped closer, and his voice dropped into something close to a command. "It belongs to my brother. I'll take it."

Logan didn't flinch, unlike the poor waitress behind him. He replied in a calm but firm tone, "I know Nico, but I don't know you. When he wakes up, you can ask him for the paper—unless the police take it into evidence. After all, we don't know what happened here."

Bruno's low growl added emphasis. The

man hesitated, then backed off, clearly unhappy.

Silence hung in the hallway until the paramedics rushed in, followed closely by Tricia. Logan got to his feet and stood beside Bruno and me, remaining there until Nico and his brother left with the paramedics.

Between the paramedics taking Nico away and Tricia asking for our statements, I completely forgot about the phone I'd kicked down the hallway. It wasn't until Tricia turned to take the waitress's statement that I started looking around for it.

"What are you—" Logan began, just as I spotted it under a bench. I crouched down to retrieve it. Bruno trotted over, sniffed the phone once, then gave it a gentle nudge with his nose as if confirming the find.

"What is that?" Tricia called from the far end of the hall.

I frowned, but stood. "I believe it's Nico's phone," I said, handing it to her, just like Logan gave her the note before.

Logan gave a low whistle. "You hid it from that jerk?"

I shrugged, uncertain. "I didn't know who he was... and honestly? He looked scary."

"I don't know if *scary* is the word," Tricia said, flipping open her notepad. "But he's definitely questionable. According to Anna—the waitress—he showed up this morning and's been yelling at Nico and the crew ever since. She thinks he's the *actual* owner of the catering company and was not happy about taking this job."

"Anna is not off," Logan said. "I heard them argument all morning. I don't think they are a happy family, if you ask me."

I closed my eyes and sighed. I'd already had doubts about Nico, but at least he'd seemed to care. Now? I wasn't so sure.

"Did you catch his name?" I asked. "I might need to talk to him about the events for this week."

Tricia's smile was tight—almost pitying. The kind that silently screamed: *good luck with that.*

"Not yet," she said. "He left with the ambulance, but I'm heading to the hospital to check on Nico. I'll send you his information once I have it."

"Thanks. That would be—"

"No." Logan cut in sharply. "Send it to me. I'll talk to him."

I glanced at him, surprised. "Logan, without Nico, I'm the one in charge of the event tonight and the catering for the weekend. I should—"

"Exactly," Logan said, deadly serious. "Which is why you should be focused on running it. Let me handle him."

"Perfect," Tricia chimed in, closing her notebook. She took a breath and shifted uncomfortably before stepping closer to Bruno.

My stomach dropped.

"Since Logan isn't currently working as an officer... technically, Bruno can't serve as one either. Not without his handler."

Bruno, sensing the shift in energy, let out a soft whine and sat down between us, his ears drooping.

"Oh... I see." I reached down and ran a hand along his back.

"Just take the vest off for now," Tricia said, looking genuinely apologetic.

Logan muttered something under his breath, then kneeled beside Bruno. He unfastened the vest and handed it over reluctantly.

"You know it's unnecessary," he told her.

"Maggie's been walking Bruno during work hours for months. Ben knows that."

"I know," Tricia said quietly, staring at the vest in her hands like it weighed more than it should. "But it's Chief Ben's call. And lately, he hasn't been thrilled. Especially this afternoon. He ordered me to check on Bruno."

Logan threw up his hands in frustration. I reached out and rested mine gently over his.

"It's okay. Bruno'll probably be happier without the vest in this heat, anyway."

Bruno gave a light wag of his tail and leaned into my leg, clearly content to stay with me—no matter what label he wore.

"It's still ridiculous," Logan muttered as Tricia walked away. "Ben knows you're more than capable of handling him. This is just him punishing me by punishing you."

I wasn't sure why Ben was being so petty either, but I did know one thing: he wasn't Chief Andrew.

"I'll talk to Ben later," I said. "But right now, can we please talk about Nico? I don't like the idea of that guy—his brother—being in charge now, and—"

Logan stepped in front of me and shook his head. "You were on your way to your office, remember?"

I rolled my eyes. "I was, but—"

"Let me handle this," he said firmly. "Like I told Tricia, I'm running this place now. You've got your own investigation. Focus on that."

"I'm about to lose my caterer! Are *you* going to explain that to Lucy?"

"If I have to, yes." His tone softened. "That guy is bad news, Maggie. Let me deal with him. Please. I'll call you as soon as I know anything. And send me the photo of the necklace so I can ask Dana."

Too many things had gone wrong in the past week for me to ignore Logan's instincts now. Even Bruno seemed to agree—he nudged Logan gently, like casting his vote.

So I didn't argue. I just walked out, Logan at my side, and Bruno close behind—my mind spinning with too many questions and a growing sense that Nico and his brother were a bigger part of this mess than I'd originally thought.

Chapter 16

T hank goodness nothing else had piled up at the office. Linda had the usual stack of paperwork waiting for me, and we even managed to go over the preliminary budget presentation for the council. It was the first moment all day that felt remotely normal.

I was still waiting to hear back from Sandie with a photo of the necklace. Knowing Lucy, I wasn't surprised she had kept my sister busy. And of course, I hadn't heard from Logan yet either—not that silence from him ever meant calm.

Sophie had just finished confirming what she'd uncovered: the former caterers had been hiding profits from the restaurant. After a call with the city lawyer, it was decided we wouldn't press charges. Legally, they had stolen nothing from the city, and the golf course hadn't missed out on any promised projects or investments.

Still, I could already hear Pat's complaints echoing in my head. From his point of view, the course never got improvements simply because there was "no money." He wouldn't enjoy hearing the money had been there the whole time—just hidden.

Especially not with the deadline to find a new caterer and restaurant manager right around the corner.

"Your presence is requested in the Mayor's office," Norman announced from the doorway.

I let out a sigh that sank my shoulders halfway into the chair. "Can you tell him I'm not here?"

Norman chuckled. "Let's just get there before Potter shows up."

We made it down the hallway faster than I'd ever moved toward the Mayor's office. My pulse only slowed when I saw that the only other person inside was Martin.

"Margaret," Mayor Dosal said from behind his desk, "how are we going to convince Detective Forest to stay and run the country club?"

I stopped mid-step. "Excuse me?"

"I just had lunch over there," he continued, gesturing vaguely toward the window. "And there's no way we can lose this menu."

My hand flew to my chest, relief crashing into me like a wave. For a second, I thought he was about to ask me to fire Logan.

"You don't want Detective Forest," I said quickly. "You want to keep Larry O'Leary and Felix Collingwood. They're the ones behind the food."

The Mayor looked pleased—until Martin cleared his throat.

"That won't be possible," Martin said, already sounding tired. "Our policy doesn't allow individuals to sign up as contractors."

"We hire individuals all the time," the Mayor countered. "None of our youth sports coaches are part of a company."

"Yes, but the city treats the restaurant differently," Martin replied, rubbing his face. "It's considered a single service under contract, not a facility with individual job roles. If we start splitting it up, we'd have to restructure personnel budgets, insurance classifications, even benefit eligibility."

The Mayor's fingers began tapping his desk in quick, agitated bursts. "We can't lose those two, Martin. The food is fantastic. You know how awful it used to be. We talked about replacing them once the contract ended, remember? This is our opportunity."

"May I suggest something?" I offered. When both men looked at me, I continued, "Why not invite the other council members for a round of golf followed by lunch? If the council likes what they see, they might change the rules for them—or wait until they're officially a corporation."

"But neither Larry nor Felix are certified chefs," Martin pointed out.

"True," I nodded, "but that's what makes it an extraordinary circumstance. These residents stepped up and volunteered when we were in crisis. I'm sure the council could grant temporary approval while they work toward certification."

The Mayor's face broke into a grin. "I like it. Martin, let's organize a 'friendly' gathering at the course this week."

Martin didn't argue, but he clearly wasn't thrilled. It wasn't until we were back in the hallway that he turned to me.

"Who's going to run the finances for the restaurant?"

I pressed my lips together. "Well... we'll

figure that part out. And we still have to convince Larry and Felix to actually take the offer —if it happens."

From behind us, Norman chuckled. When I turned to give him a look, he lifted his hands innocently.

"I'm just glad I kept my mouth shut for once."

I was about to reply when my phone buzzed twice. Two texts from Sandie.

The first was a photo—Lucy, mid-laugh, clearly posing for a candid shot. The necklace was visible, though barely. Still, I hoped it was enough for Dana to work her magic.

The second message was in all capital letters:

YOU BETTER GET TO MOM'S RIGHT NOW!

It wasn't even 5:15 yet. Whatever it was, Lucy clearly wasn't happy—and my gut told me Sandie was the one paying the price.

Bruno trotted over to me with his tail low, sensing the shift.

"Come on, buddy," I whispered. "Looks like we're in a bit of a mess."

Bruno had just curled up in the passenger seat —finally comfortable and halfway to snoring— when my phone rang. This time, it wasn't Sandie.

"Hi, Logan," I said as I climbed into the car and started the engine. "Did you get the picture?"

"You know how weird it is to send a photo of my ex-girlfriend to my ex-wife?"

I instinctively hit the brake harder than I meant to—luckily, no one was behind me.

"Oh boy... when you put it like that, it sounds complicated. Was Dana mad?"

Logan chuckled. "Not really. I mean, considering you solved the murder of her boyfriend, she can't be too picky."

I shook my head and glanced at Bruno. His ears flicked, likely picking up on my tension. Life had been a mess lately. A spring full of crime. *Murder* kind. And summer wasn't even halfway over.

"Anyway," Logan continued, "Dana said she'll check it out tomorrow morning."

I let out a sigh. "Not ideal, but at least someone's looking into it. Any word from Nico?"

"Yes, ma'am." Logan's tone shifted. "He

called the country club. And I had the distinct pleasure of meeting Pat's fame."

"Oh no! How'd that go?"

Logan puffed out a breath. I could practically hear him rubbing his face or rolling his eyes—maybe both.

"Let's just say he was very glad to hear I'm only temporary. Poor Nico called from the hospital, and this guy Potter kept pressuring him to come back to work. There's definitely some history there."

"How's Nico doing?"

There was a pause, followed by a heavier sigh. "Well... he claims he passed out because he forgot to monitor his sugar. Says he just fell down the stairs. No broken bones, but the hospital's keeping him overnight."

"You don't believe him?"

It took a beat too long for him to answer.

"The paramedics noted some bruising—arms and knuckles. Sure, he could've hit the wall or railings on the way down. But from what Tricia heard from the waitress, Anna... we both think there might've been a struggle with his brother Ralph, the guy we met in the hallway."

Bruno let out a low whine. I reached out

and scratched behind his ears, unsure if I was comforting him or myself.

"If he was arguing with his brother like Anna said," I murmured, "maybe they fought. Maybe he's just covering for Ralph?"

"I think so too," Logan replied. Then his voice faded, replaced by the sound of footsteps and muffled voices.

"Sorry," he said when he returned. "Had to tell Felix how to set the tablecloths."

That got my attention. "What tablecloths? The restaurant doesn't use them."

"I kind of... volunteered to help this Ralph Henson with tonight's dinner."

Bruno sat up straighter in his seat, tail thumping once. Even he knew that didn't sound right.

"Is Ralph dangerous?" I whispered, even though we were still alone.

I could hear Logan rake a hand through his hair. Not a good sign.

"We don't know. Tricia isn't sure either. No criminal record, but there was a civil suit— negligence and fraud. Looked like it got dropped last year."

"Dropped as in *settled*?"

His voice dropped. "No... dropped as in the other party vanished."

My stomach twisted just as I pulled up in front of my mom's house. "I'll talk to Lucy. Maybe we cancel dinner."

"I don't think anyone at the wedding party is in danger," he said gently. "But that's why I'm here. And Tricia's going to act as host. Whatever you do, don't blow her cover, okay?"

I nodded instinctively, then remembered I was on speaker. "I won't."

Bruno let out a low bark—not at anything in particular, just the kind he made when something felt off but not wrong *yet*.

"I'll see you soon," I said. Then, before I could hang up, Logan added—

"Maggie... see if you can bring Darcy. I've got an idea."

Chapter 17

My sister didn't even wait for me to finish opening the door before she started yelling.

"Where have you been? Lucy is in full panic mode! You didn't even try on the dresses?"

I stepped inside with Bruno trotting in right behind me, tail wagging like he had no idea we were walking straight into a domestic storm.

Paul sat in the living room, doing a poor job of hiding his amusement, while Toby was deeply focused on building a tower of blocks on the coffee table. Sure enough, Bruno ditched me and went to sniff around the blocks. After giving Toby a friendly nudge, he sat down next to my nephew, ready to assist.

"What dresses?" I asked, instantly realizing I'd picked the wrong hill to die on.

Sandie threw her arms in the air dramatically, pacing like she was rehearsing for a courtroom drama. "The bridesmaid dress, Maggie! The one you're wearing at the wedding on Saturday! And the one for the rehearsal tomorrow?"

Paul burst out laughing—until Sandie turned and glared. He coughed into his hand and turned toward the strange block tower like it had just become fascinating.

"Sandie, I've been working. I didn't have time for—"

"Mommy!" Darcy's voice rang out from the kitchen. She ran in full speed and launched herself at me like a tiny, curly-haired rocket.

"I missed you so much!" she cried as I caught her in a hug.

"I missed you, sunflower." I kissed her cheek and spun her once before setting her down. "Did you have dinner yet?"

Darcy shook her head. "Grandma's cooking. With Ben. Bruno will be helping."

Bruno, as if on cue, gave a soft bark and padded over to us, nosing Darcy's arm before sitting beside her like the loyal sidekick he was. She leaned into him, patting his head and whispering something only he could hear. His ears perked.

Sandie still looked like she was ready to lecture me into next week. "You have a dinner tonight, Maggie."

"I remember that one," I said, brushing a curl out of Darcy's face. "But there's been a change of plans."

Before Sandie could fire off another round, I added, "The caterer is a mess. Logan's stepping in. I'll explain while I try on the other two dresses. They're here, right?"

Sandie let out a long, exhausted breath and started climbing the stairs. "Yes. I brought them here. I knew you wouldn't go to the rental house with Lucy."

I smiled at her retreating back. "You know me too well."

Then I turned to Darcy and took both of her little hands in mine. "Would you like to come to dinner with me tonight? You'll need to wear one of your fancy dresses."

Her eyes lit up instantly, like I'd asked her to be princess of the evening. "Really? Can Bruno come too?"

I looked at Bruno, who tilted his head with hopeful eyes, clearly picking up on his name.

"Well," I said, lowering my voice like we

were making a secret pact, "if Bruno can behave like the gentleman he is... he might get invited."

Darcy squealed and hugged his neck. "He's the best gentleman!"

Right then, Mom appeared in the kitchen doorway, towel in hand, clearly having caught enough of the conversation to give me *the* look —the one that said she was unimpressed and definitely on Sandie's side.

"Logan needs her," I said, gesturing toward myself, my tone apologetic but firm.

It was the truth. As far as I knew.

Bruno gave a soft *woof*, like he was backing me up.

And honestly? That was enough.

The dinner had originally been scheduled for one of the rooms upstairs, but after losing our caterer—and then Nico—we were reassigned to a smaller room near the restaurant on the first floor. Personally, I thought it was an up-grade. The view was better, and the access to the patio and fire pit gave it extra charm. But I wasn't the bride. And Lucy was not pleased.

"This isn't what we agreed on!" she yelled at Pat the moment I stepped inside with Darcy and Bruno at my side. "You said everything was handled and that my wedding wouldn't be affected by your problems!"

Part of me was tempted to record her—just to show Linda that someone finally yelled at Pat—but I knew better. Instead, I tightened my hold on Darcy's hand and walked toward the chaos.

"Our new caterer had a medical emergency," Pat said, his voice surprisingly apologetic. "He'll be back tomorrow—"

"It's not my fault your staff has health issues!" Lucy snapped, crossing her arms. "I'm not paying for this mess."

I was about to chime in—something along the lines of *then feel free to leave*—when a deep voice cut through the room like a dropped piano.

"What seems to be the problem, Miss Clover?"

Everyone turned. Ralph Henson stood in the doorway, his frame so large it blocked most of the light behind him. Bruno stiffened beside me, his tail rising slightly and his body shifting just in front of Darcy, as if shielding her. She squeezed my hand so tightly I heard my knuckles pop and tried to tuck herself behind me.

In front of me, Lucy's face went pale. Across the room, Johnathan took a step forward, but it was Louis who answered, striding confidently toward us.

"I'm sure Lucy here is just disappointed about not using the upstairs terrace," he said smoothly, pausing beside her. "But we'll adjust the photoshoot. I heard the new chef is the best thing that's happened to this club in years."

Pat chuckled—probably thinking that would lighten the mood—but Ralph turned a slow, unimpressed look on him. Just like that, the cocky coach ducked his head and slinked out of the room.

"You can still take pictures upstairs," Ralph said, staring down at Lucy, whose posture had crumpled into silence. "My brother had a medical emergency. That's why the location changed. He'll be back tomorrow. Everything will be back on track."

He didn't wait for a response. He turned and walked away, the murmur of confused voices swelling behind him.

I watched him go, unsettled. Even though I'd seen the whole thing, I couldn't shake the feeling that I'd missed something important.

"Are you all right?" I heard Louis ask, and I assumed he was talking to Lucy.

"Mom?" Darcy whispered, tugging on my sleeve. Only then did I realize Louis's eyes were on *me*.

"Me?" I cleared my throat. "Yes. Perfectly fine."

Louis gave one of his signature grins and turned his attention to Darcy. "You're just as beautiful as your mom."

Darcy shifted closer to me but managed a shy, "Thank you." Bruno sniffed Louis's shoes once, then sat squarely between us, his silent opinion loud and clear.

Before I could say anything else, Sandie joined us with a frown. "Who is that man?"

"That's exactly what we're trying to find out," Logan said behind me, his voice calm but commanding. His presence was like opening a window in a stuffy room. I didn't even realize I'd been holding my breath.

Lucy, now recovered, stomped toward him like a storm cloud. "What are *you* doing here?" she demanded, surprisingly quiet but no less furious.

I could've stepped in—could've explained why he was here. But... I kind of wanted to see this.

Logan stayed composed. "I'm helping my dear friend. And I needed my professional taste-tester."

Before Lucy could get another word in, Logan crouched down to Darcy's level, lowering his voice. But I still caught every word.

"I need to sneak into a room," he said. "And you're the only one small and brave enough to help. I'll pay you... in ice cream. Or one of those fruity things you like."

Darcy lit up. "Pavlova?"

"Pavlova," Logan confirmed with a solemn nod.

She grinned wide, let go of my hand, and looked up at me with sparkling eyes. "I'll be back, Mommy!"

Bruno gave a soft bark, clearly not liking being left out. Logan gave him a look. "I'll need you too, officer. Think you're up for it?"

Bruno's tail wagged once, then he stood at Darcy's side, walking off with her like her personal guard.

I watched them go, my protective instincts tugging at me—but somehow, I wasn't worried. Not with Logan at her side.

That said more than I wanted to admit out loud.

Chapter 18

I watched Darcy wave at me from the far end of the hallway, her smile so wide it lifted something in my chest. Bruno trotted beside her, alert and proud, clearly taking his role as escort very seriously. Logan gave me a small smirk before turning the corner with them, and I wasn't the only one who noticed.

Lucy, standing stiffly at my side, grabbed my arm and yanked me toward the wall.

"Hey—" I protested, stumbling into a side table. "You don't have to drag me."

She didn't stop until we were tucked in a corner, out of earshot. Her eyes burned into me.

"What is *he* doing here?" she hissed. "You

told him, didn't you? I said I didn't want the police involved—especially not that traitor."

I pulled my arm free and steadied myself with a breath. "First of all, he's not a traitor. And if this is about prom again—"

"How can you just forgive him, Maggie?"

I started to turn away. I wasn't going to argue with her about high school drama tonight. But her next question made me pause.

"Did he keep talking to you?"

"What?"

"After everything—with his mom getting sick, after he ghosted me—did he still talk to you?"

I opened my mouth, but she didn't wait.

"Don't pretend. Be honest. Did he reach out after we broke up?"

"You and Sandie banned him from the house! What was he supposed to—"

"Oh, come on," she snapped. "You saw him at school. Did he try? No. He shut everyone out—including you. And that wasn't on me or Sandie. That was him."

I folded my arms, heat prickling the back of my neck. Across the room, I spotted Sandie moving toward us, probably catching the tension from a mile away.

"I'm serious, Margaret," Lucy pressed,

voice rising. "I don't want him here. He needs to go."

That did it.

"He's staying," I said evenly. I wasn't going to raise my voice. I didn't need to. "And for the record, he's not here for you—he's helping me. With *my* actual job. As Director of Recreation and Parks. Not with your supposedly missing necklace."

Lucy's cheeks flushed, but her voice dropped to a mutter. "I didn't misplace it."

Before she could say more, Sandie appeared and gently slid an arm through hers.

"Maggie," she said softly, "Julia Cullens just got here."

The quiet plea in her tone reminded me why I was in heels, at a dinner, on a Thursday night.

I gave Sandie a faint smile—my way of saying I was done, and maybe even sorry she had to be the buffer.

"I'll see if I can talk to her," I said, turning away without a glance at Lucy.

Finding Julia Cullens was the easy part. Her white hair, arranged in a perfect bun, the string of pearls around her neck, and her elegant navy-blue dress—impeccably suited for a woman in her nineties—made her practically glow from every corner of the room.

The hard part was actually talking to her.

Walking up and saying hello was no problem. But getting a quiet moment with her? Nearly impossible.

"Have you been hiding?" Louis asked, stepping squarely into my path just as I made my move toward Julia. He smiled, but something about it felt too polished, too deliberate. He held out a glass of white wine, and although his tone was warm, his eyes flicked briefly over my shoulder before locking back onto mine—like he was watching more than just me.

"I brought the good stuff," he added, almost like a bribe.

If I had to confess something, it's that I'm not a wine drinker. Beer? Occasionally. Fancy wine? Not so much—unless it's frozen. I know, it's too sweet for most people, but for someone whose favorite food is ice cream, it's perfection.

Unfortunately, the glass in my hand was *not* frozen wine. I offered a polite smile and took the tiniest sip when Louis raised his glass.

Bruno, who had stayed close at my side like a furry shadow, gave a low huff, tail swishing once. I rested a hand on his back, glad for his solid, silent company.

"I must say," Louis began, his voice light as he glanced toward Lucy and Johnathan entering from the gazebo, "I'm surprised you didn't lose your spot in the wedding party."

"Hopefully you didn't lose any bets on it," I replied, keeping my tone dry.

He looked back at me with faux innocence. "I would never make such a terrible bet," he said smoothly. "You're by far the most interesting person in this room."

I nearly choked on my wine, swallowing hard to keep from coughing. I prayed he didn't notice the heat creeping up my neck.

"I'm not so sure about that," I muttered.

He didn't step closer, but somehow, he felt *closer*. The way he looked at me—direct, appraising—made the hairs on the back of my neck lift. Not in the good way. Something about it wasn't flirtation. It was *calculation*.

"Oh, you are," he continued. "You've got the charm, a sweet daughter, a K-9 sidekick"—he gave Bruno a slight nod—"and you're Director of Parks and Recreation."

I cleared my throat and did something utterly stupid: I corrected him.

"Recreation and Parks," I said. When he tilted his head in amusement, I added, "Recreation is first. Not like the show."

His smile widened, but it didn't reach his eyes this time.

"Of course. How could I forget? That's why you're in charge of this club and its golf course. Do you know how deep those ponds are?"

His strange question had me frowning in confusion, but he quickly added, "I'm not a golf champion. I'd be devastated to lose anything valuable. I was so close the other morning! How bad would it have been on hole 9? The one by the restaurant, right?"

He offered his arm, but before I could think of an excuse, salvation barreled in.

"Mommy!"

Darcy slammed into my waist like a miniature whirlwind, her voice echoing across the room. I dropped to my knees and hugged her tight. My relief was instant. Sweet and sincere.

"How did it go? And where did you go?" I asked, brushing a wisp of hair from her forehead.

She tried for seriousness, but the joy in her

voice gave her away. "Logan told me not to say anything until we get home."

She pointed toward the entrance. Sure enough, Logan was standing there with a posture too casual to be relaxed. His expression was all focus—until Darcy waved. Then it softened, like someone turned the lights back on behind his eyes.

Still, his gaze flicked to Louis. He didn't smile. Didn't blink either.

I stood, ready to walk over to him, but a waitress intercepted us.

"Please take your seats," she said with a professional smile. "Dinner will be served shortly."

Logan didn't move. Louis, however, raised his glass again in mock salute as I turned back toward the tables. Bruno let out another quiet huff, pressing against my side like he didn't like the vibe either.

"Come on, boy," I whispered, giving his ears a scratch as I guided Darcy toward our seats. "Stay close."

Chapter 19

If Louis was right about anything, it was about my amazing daughter. I didn't know exactly what Logan had plotted with her, but I had a feeling it was something similar to what I'd planned to do between the soup and the chicken.

"You see that lady over there, Darcy?" I leaned close to her ear and, from under the table, pointed subtly toward Julia Cullens.

Darcy straightened up in her chair and scanned the room. When her eyes landed on the perfectly coiffed white hair across the room, she grinned. Just as she opened her mouth—probably to shout—I whispered again.

"I need you to walk over there and wait for Bruno."

She frowned with the same seriousness she

used when deciding which ice cream flavor to pick, then said in a too-grown-up tone, "You need an excuse to talk to that lady in private, don't you, Mommy?"

I nodded. That only made her giggle.

"That's all right. I like to help you. And Logan. And Grandma."

"Grandma?" I asked, raising a brow.

But Darcy was already hopping off her chair, heading straight for Julia Cullens with mission-like determination—completely ignoring my question.

Bruno had been resting behind my chair, taking in the room like a dignified guest. Seeing him out and about without his vest was a little strange—another reminder that this night wasn't exactly typical. I made a mental note to ask Ben about it later. For now, I gave a quiet pat to my leg.

Bruno perked up immediately, ears twitching, eyes on me.

"Find Darcy," I whispered.

His nose twitched, tail wagging once. Within seconds, he was up and trotting across the room with the focused ease of a seasoned sleuth. I counted a beat, then stood and followed, feigning exasperation.

"I got him!" I called to anyone startled by the sudden flurry of movement.

People around us gasped, squeaked, or murmured—because of course, a large German shepherd weaving through a dinner party would cause a stir. But Bruno ignored them all, locked in on his target. When he reached Darcy, she let out a delighted squeal and tumbled to the floor in a heap of laughter and dog kisses.

Julia Cullens turned in her chair to witness the chaos, her face unreadable. I winced inwardly. Not everyone was a fan of kids and dogs, and maybe I'd misjudged the moment.

"I'm so sorry," I said as I reached them, pretending to struggle as I tried to separate Bruno from a very giggly Darcy. "He's in training. A work in progress."

Julia's eyes lingered on us, cool and composed. I held my breath.

"I always wanted a dog," she said, her voice a bit raspy, then turned toward the table. "Did you ever want one, Theodore?"

I glanced up and noticed Theodore approaching from the far side of the table, but she didn't wait for his response. This time, she looked directly at me.

"My father swore they were untamable and

messy. Still..." Her features softened as she looked at Darcy. "What's your friend's name?"

Darcy, still on the floor with Bruno's big head resting in her lap, replied cheerfully, "Bruno! And this is my mommy."

That single sentence seemed to change something in Julia. Her elegant posture relaxed, and her eyes warmed with a sweetness only the very old or very young can offer.

"It's lovely to meet you, Bruno and Mommy," she said. "And you are?"

"Oh, right!" Darcy scrambled up, brushing dog fur from her dress. She gave a little curtsey. "I'm Darcy Willow."

"Well, very nice to meet you, Darcy Willow. I'm Julia Cullens—but you can call me Jules."

Darcy nodded seriously. "Do you want to pet him? He's super sweet and won't jump on you. He only does that to me, or Logan, or criminals. Sometimes Mommy. And maybe Toby. But he won't do it to you."

Julia let out a soft chuckle and turned in her chair to reach out a hand. Darcy gave Bruno a quick command, and—just like that— he approached slowly, sniffed Julia's fingers, and sat beside her with that gentle tilt of the head he reserved for polite introductions.

After a brief hesitation, Julia's hand settled

on his fur, and something changed in her expression. Not just a smile—something deeper. A small memory, maybe. A younger version of herself peeking through.

"Would you care to join us—me?" she asked, her hand still resting on Bruno's head. "I believe Theodore is ready to socialize with people who are a little more fun."

"You're the fun one, Granny," Theodore said, his tone surprisingly sweet as he leaned down to kiss the top of her head.

It was hard to reconcile him with the immature, mischievous man from the day before. Even the tattoos on his arms, which yesterday had seemed brash, now gave him a certain character—something grounded.

"Nonsense," Julia replied, still petting Bruno. "I saw you eyeing the girl near the patio door. I may be losing my eyesight, but I'd bet she's quite pretty."

Theodore chuckled. "For the record, you're the prettiest girl in the room. Though it does sound like you're kicking me out."

"I am," she said with a little roll of her eyes, then looked at me. "But not you girls. That boy needs to enjoy his youth—and more importantly, let me breathe for a bit."

"I noticed he didn't want to leave your

side," I said, taking the seat across from her after Theodore left.

Julia sighed. "He thinks it's his fault I ended up in my current situation. My sweet boy. All heart, not quite enough logic."

I nodded slowly, then met her gaze. "Are you in some kind of trouble?"

She looked at me for a long moment, her hand still lightly stroking Bruno's fur. Then she exhaled and asked softly:

"Do you like stories?"

Darcy sat beside me, happily nibbling on a second cookie while Julia Cullens told us her story. Bruno lay sprawled at our feet, his head resting on his paws but his ears twitching now and then, like he was listening too.

"My father was a forest ranger in Poland, many years ago," Julia began. Her eyes grew glassy, but her voice remained steady. "Russia wasn't always part of the Alliance during the war. When they took over Poland, they exiled all government employees and their families. Ours ended up in Siberia."

The thought of being sent to a prison

camp just for doing your job made my stomach tighten. I instinctively reached for Darcy's arm, wanting to pull her close and hold her, but she was still listening intently—her brow slightly furrowed.

"That must have been awful," I said softly.

Julia shrugged gently. "I don't remember much of it. I was very young. I remember being cold. And my mother—she was always sad. My father used to be funny. He tried to make us laugh, even there."

Bruno let out a low, content sigh and shifted closer to Darcy's chair, as if offering her some extra warmth in response to the chill of the story. She reached down absentmindedly to stroke the fur between his ears.

"The Alliance eventually forced Russia to release Poland and its citizens in exchange for help. My father didn't want to return, didn't want anything to do with the war. So we left. My mother had family in Mexico, and that's where we went."

Even Darcy had stopped eating now, her hands resting still in her lap.

"That's where we met Lady Victoria Fernández," Julia continued, her voice brightening slightly. "She used to tell us stories about Spanish royalty. About balls and tea parties before the first war. Her family had left Europe long ago, and by the time I met her, she was the last of them."

Darcy shifted in her seat and reached over, nudging my arm gently before climbing onto my lap without a word.

"Are you okay, sweetie?" I whispered.

"It's a sad story," Darcy said, her voice quiet but clear.

Julia gave her a warm smile. "Would you like me to stop?"

Darcy shook her head and straightened. "Oh no. I want to know what happened to your family."

Julia chuckled and patted her hand. "In that case, I promise you, it has a happy ending."

Bruno, sensing Darcy's shift in mood, nudged her calf with his nose before settling again at our feet like a sentinel.

"My aunt had been Lady Victoria's companion since they were just a little older than you," Julia said, looking at Darcy. "By the time we arrived, my aunt was nearly the age I am now and so grateful to have us. I loved running errands, just so I could walk near the main square and pass the white-columned theater."

She paused and sighed deeply, her gaze

going soft. "It reminded me of home... before everything changed."

She patted Darcy's hand again and sat up a little straighter. "Now, for the happy part. My father got a job with a company that did a lot of business with the United States. One day, he invited a new American colleague over for dinner."

There was a twinkle in her eye now.

"I wasn't a child anymore by then—and I had never seen such a tall and interesting gentleman in my life." She gave a dreamy sigh. "Darcy, you're too young to understand this part, but your mother does." She locked eyes with me. "That flutter in your chest when someone walks into a room. That comfort in saying nothing and still feeling understood. That was Edgar Cullens."

Darcy gasped and covered her mouth with both hands. "Was that your husband?!"

Julia's entire face lit up. "Yes, it was. And believe it or not—he was Polish too. But his family had moved directly to the U.S. before the war."

"Wow!" Darcy breathed. "That is so romantic! Did you have a big wedding like this one?"

"Oh yes," Julia said, nodding. "We married

in Mexico, just before moving here. And on Saturday, you'll see my most special heirloom."

Darcy turned to me with wide eyes and a deep frown. "Heirloom? Like... a balloon?"

Julia laughed gently while I leaned in to whisper the real definition in Darcy's ear. Her little nod of understanding made my heart squeeze.

"Lady Victoria passed away a few years before the wedding," Julia continued. "She left everything to my mother, who then gave me a white gold necklace on my wedding day. It has a large blue sapphire pendant. Ever since, every bride in our family has worn it."

Julia paused and looked at Darcy. "It's how I honor where we came from. It's not just jewelry—it's memory."

She turned her gaze across the room. I followed it to find Theodore chatting animatedly with a small group near the bar.

"I don't know if I'll live long enough to see him marry," she said with a sigh. "He's all the trouble I have left in this world."

She reached across the table and rested her hand on mine. "I'm sure you understand. That little angel—" she nodded at Darcy, who was now braiding a lock of her own hair, Bruno still curled beside her "—she's your joy and your worry all at once."

I nodded, my smile hopefully steadier than I felt. Inside, I was spiraling.

She *owned* the necklace. My worry about Lucy's future mother-in-law hiding a secret disappeared. The necklace wasn't just real. It was a part of Julia's story. A piece of her soul.

The photo I'd sent Logan earlier played in my mind: the sapphire sparkling in a way that no longer just looked expensive—but meaningful. And suddenly, the price, the wedding, even Lucy's outrage didn't matter at all.

We had to find it.

Because now, it wasn't about a missing heirloom.

It was about protecting a legacy.

Chapter 20

Darcy fell asleep in the car on the way home from the dinner, which meant I had no way to interrogate her. Of course, I also couldn't find Logan after my chat with Julia—or while struggling to pull Bruno away from all the guests feeding him scraps like he was the guest of honor.

"No dinner for you, mister," I muttered to Bruno as I turned onto my mom's street. The sight of Logan's truck parked in front of the house sent a wave of relief—and a flutter of nervousness—through me.

After pulling into the driveway, I opened the back door to let Bruno out first. He leaped down with enthusiasm and bounded up the porch steps like it was his personal runway. Only then did I notice Logan standing there, hand in his pocket, his sling still around one shoulder. He gave me a crooked smile and a little shrug.

"No one's home," he said.

I should've guessed. Paul had taken Toby, and Ben was in the house when we left. It wasn't like my mom not to be here, but honestly? I was glad she was out enjoying herself. I'd still be having a talk with her, though—she could've warned me.

I reached into the back seat to lift Darcy. Her eyes fluttered open for a second before her head dropped onto my shoulder again.

Logan jogged down the steps. "Let me help you."

I opened my mouth to protest—his arm was still healing—but he carefully gathered Darcy in his good arm like she weighed nothing. She blinked up at him, recognized his face, and snuggled into his neck, her arms draping sleepily around him.

Bruno padded alongside us all the way to the front door, pausing only to give a suspicious sniff toward a potted plant. Once inside, he trotted ahead as if inspecting the house for any intruders—or hidden snacks.

I followed Logan down the hall to Darcy's room and watched from the doorway as he gently set her down and tucked the blanket around her. She barely stirred.

Something warm and unexpected swelled in my chest. The ease with which he cared for her, the gentleness—it meant more to me than I could explain.

"Do you want some tea?" I asked, but didn't wait for his answer.

In the kitchen, Bruno lay curled up by the pantry, his head resting over his front paws but his eyes still alert, keeping watch. Logan sat at the counter while I filled the kettle.

"So," I said, glancing over my shoulder, "Darcy said you told her to wait until we got home before she told me what you two did?"

Logan's eyes lit up with that spark I recognized too well. "I should wait until she's awake so she can tell you herself."

I leaned against the counter and narrowed my eyes. "If you don't tell me, I'm not sharing what Julia told me about the necklace."

He lifted a brow, unfazed. "That's not part of my investigation. I can wait."

"Just tell me!" I groaned.

He smirked but finally gave in. "I showed Darcy a little secret you've been keeping... about a certain golf championship and who won it."

Of all the possibilities I'd imagined, that was not one of them.

"What?"

He grinned wider. "So you don't deny it?"

"Deny what?" But I could already tell by the look on his face that I'd walked right into it. "The championship? It was a high school one."

"You didn't mention it when I asked you about playing golf."

"I told you I used to play. That doesn't mean I'm still good at it."

Logan leaned forward, his voice low. "You know how many hockey tournaments our school won when I was playing. You were at most of them. If you'd invited me to your tournament, I would've been there."

"To a golf match?"

"Sure. Why not?"

I couldn't help laughing. "You clearly don't play golf."

"Maybe not. But that doesn't mean I wouldn't have supported you." His voice softened. "Up until those last months of senior year, your family was like mine."

Lucy's earlier words echoed in my head, and a strange tightness pinched at my chest. The kettle whistled behind me, and I turned quickly to pour the hot water—happy for the distraction.

"Why didn't you talk to me after you and Lucy—" I stopped myself. "No, forget it. Doesn't matter." I sighed and moved back to his question. "I didn't invite anyone," I muttered. "Most of the matches were early. They were hard to follow. My mom yelled at me about it too."

"I would have come to your game if you had told me," he said quietly and picked up his cup. "And if you ever play again, I'd love to come."

"You might regret that," I said, trying to lighten the mood again. He gave me a small smile and, thankfully, changed the subject.

"Anyway, besides Darcy's golf history lesson, I used the opportunity to snoop around Potter's desk."

I blinked. "You used Darcy as a cover to get into his office?"

"She was never in danger. And Pat loves showing off his accomplishments."

"His accomplishments?"

"Yes," Logan said, taking a sip of tea. "I asked to see old team photos and focused on praising him, not the players. Worked like a charm."

I raised a brow. "He just let you in?"

Logan grinned. "Let's just say there was also a loud crash in the hallway and a fake drunk golfer trying to get into the storage room. Courtesy of Felix."

I burst out laughing. "I wish I'd seen that."

"In any case," Logan said, growing serious again, "you were right to suspect Nico."

I stood a little straighter. "Go on."

"Pat coached Nico last summer. Told me he only knew him casually, but I found an email from Pat to Nico, asking him to review the spreadsheets from your previous caterer and 'point out any inconsistencies.'"

I frowned. "Why would he—?"

Logan cut me off with a smile. "Then Nico replied asking to meet this past Monday. Called it 'a great solution to our problems.'"

"Our problems? What problems does Nico have? His brother?"

Before Logan could respond, the front door opened. My mom stepped inside mid-laugh, with Ben right behind her.

"Maggie!" she said brightly, startled but cheerful. "You're home early—and with Logan."

It wasn't accusatory, but the room froze for a beat as Ben and Logan locked eyes.

Ben cleared his throat. "I better go, Lucretia. It was a lovely night."

Logan stood up smoothly, never missing a beat. "I was leaving too. Maybe we can walk out together—and you can finally explain what your problem is with me?"

The tension snapped like a rubber band. My mom's eyes widened, and I was too stunned to stop it.

Ben gave Logan a sharp look and replied with an edge to his voice. "After you, Forest."

Bruno, who had lifted his head the moment the door opened, gave a soft *whuff* and trotted between the two men—his tail held high like he was reminding them that the real protector of the house was still on duty.

Chapter 21

Friday, daytime...

L inda had a big, satisfied smile on her face when I walked into the department the next morning. I didn't even have to ask. News in Apple Creek traveled faster than Wi-Fi.

"I heard what happened last night," she said, handing me a steaming cup of coffee.

"Where's the pile of paperwork I'm supposed to sign?" I asked, though I still took the coffee.

She rolled her eyes, but the grin didn't leave her face. "Oh, it's coming. But I wasn't about to ruin this magnificent morning with budget spreadsheets."

As we walked toward my office, I finally had to ask. The vague idea I had didn't seem nearly exciting enough to justify her delight.

"What exactly happened last night?"

"Your sister's friend humiliated Pat Potter. Before dinner."

I nodded, but Linda wasn't done.

"And Pat had it coming for years. Years, Maggie! I just wish someone had recorded it and posted it for the world to see."

If there was one thing I'd learned over the last few days, it was that Pat Potter was... not beloved. I still didn't understand all the reasons why, but clearly, I needed to.

"Can I ask—why do you dislike him so much?"

Linda huffed and planted her hands on her hips. "I'm not going to let you ruin this moment for me, Margaret. That man deserved what he got."

"I'm not trying to ruin anything, I promise," I said, hands raised. "It's just... well, it's not just you. Mr. Elliott, Terry, and a handful of others really don't like him either. It feels personal."

Linda crossed her arms, her tone lowering. "A lifetime ago, Agnes O'Leary, Gladis Williams, Terry's wife—Martha—and I used to play golf every Monday. Just a little group of us ladies."

"That's actually pretty cool. Why did you—?"

"Potter!" she snapped. "When he got promoted to head pro, he made it his mission to 'eliminate less-than-average players' from the course." She even used finger quotes. "We weren't great—never said we were—but we always played the last tee, didn't slow anyone down, and left quietly. It was our summer thing. He turned it into a nightmare."

I had a good idea of what she meant. As one of his former students, I knew Pat's teaching "style" leaned heavily on criticism and humiliation. Not exactly the spirit of good sportsmanship.

"So you all just... stopped playing?"

Linda's expression darkened. "Eventually. And we weren't the only ones. Mr. Elliott and Terry used to hit the driving range and grab lunch. But Pat made it clear they weren't welcome either. Said if you weren't playing a full round, you didn't belong. And the worst part? The course started bringing in more money, so the Council turned a blind eye."

I leaned against my desk and pushed my hair back, trying to control my rising frustration. Of course it brought in more money. I'd been around when the school district added golf to the curriculum. That alone brought youth tournaments and traffic. Pat may have been the professional face of it, but I doubted he was the reason for the boom.

"This makes me so angry," I said. "No one should be bullied out of a space they love—especially by the person in charge of it. Pat's either changing his ways or leaving. I promise you that, Linda."

She didn't respond right away. Her expression stayed neutral, like she'd heard promises before. But none of those promises had come from me.

"You'll see," I added. "In the meantime, could you call Pat for me? Let him know I'd like him to write a handwritten apology to Miss Glover for last night—and he'll personally cover the extra costs for changing the venue."

Linda blinked. "I thought the caterer was covering the extra costs?"

I leaned in and dropped my voice. "They are. But he doesn't need to know that. He should feel this in his wallet."

My office phone rang.

"You take that," Linda said, already walking toward her desk. "I've got a call to make."

I heard her delighted laughter as I picked up the phone.

"Hello?"

"You're onto something," Logan said on the other end. From the engine hum in the background, I could tell he was driving.

Logan was already sitting at the far table in the bakery when I arrived, about ten minutes after his call. He hadn't said much over the phone, but there'd been just enough urgency in his voice to make me press the gas pedal harder than I probably should have.

Bruno rode in the passenger seat, alert the whole way there, occasionally letting out a soft whine—like he could tell something important was brewing.

"I got you a blueberry muffin," Logan said, standing to pull out the chair for me as I walked in. "Hope that's okay. I have a vague memory that you like them."

"Of course I like them," I said, sliding into the seat. "But let's be honest—there's nothing in this bakery I wouldn't like."

He smiled, and I noticed that instead of a

muffin, a mostly eaten slice of pavlova sat on his plate.

"Is that a—?"

"What's left of a pavlova?" he nodded. "Yes. I blame Darcy for it."

Bruno sat obediently at my feet, but I felt him shift slightly, ever so subtly pressing against my leg. I gave his head a little scratch under the table.

"How did things go with Ben?" I asked as I unwrapped the muffin. The smell of warm butter and blueberries tried to distract me, but I kept my eyes on Logan. His expression froze for a second before he leaned back.

"I think... fine? Maybe. Who knows."

"What do you mean? He's like your father."

Logan let out a dry chuckle and shook his head. "I have a father, you know?"

I waved the comment away. "Of course. But Ben's your mentor, right?"

He sighed and looked up at the ceiling for a moment, like it might hold the answers. Bruno let out a soft huff, as if echoing his frustration.

"Ben's upset because he thinks I put your life in danger. And if he's anyone's adoptive parent, it's yours. He doesn't want your mom worried or upset at him."

"My life? You didn't put my life in danger. If anything, you're always trying to keep me out of trouble."

He looked at me, eyes suddenly somber. "You've nearly been killed twice, Maggie. He's not wrong to be concerned."

I reached across the table and placed my hand over his. "You're the one who got shot. And you saved me—both times."

His fingers closed gently around mine. For a moment, the rest of the bakery faded into the background. The air between us shifted, warm and still. The butterflies in my stomach went completely rogue.

"I'd get shot for you any day," he said softly.

Then he let go and leaned back, the moment slipping away like steam off coffee.

"Ben thinks you were involved in the heist investigation I had with Arthur," he added, tone tight again. "He nearly fired Arthur, but he can't afford to lose his ME."

"What?!" I sat straighter, heat rising in my chest. "That's ridiculous! I'm going to apologize to Arthur and have a serious talk with Ben. He can't—"

Logan reached out, gently waving me down. "Please don't. This is why I didn't want to tell you. Ben's just... trying to look out for you. So am I."

I crossed my arms and frowned. "Where did he even get that idea?"

"I think your mom overheard something you and Sandie were talking about. Plus, Arthur mentioned you'd been in the office... It doesn't matter." He changed the subject quickly. "Bruno should get his vest back on Monday, and I'll be back on duty the week after."

He raised a hand before I could object. "And yes, I'm still helping you with the Country Club and Lucy's necklace."

He didn't give me time to argue.

"I talked to Dana. You were right—something's off with the missing necklace."

My heart skipped. Julia's story had changed the way I felt about the necklace's importance. "Actually... I think I was wrong," I said quietly.

"Yes, you were," Logan replied quickly, with a little too much enthusiasm. "The Cullens are the original owners. Dana traced it— Lady Victoria Fernandez gave it to Julia Galecki, who later became Julia Cullens after her marriage."

Relief swept through me. "So what's the issue, then?"

Logan slid a paper across the table. "Apparently, this isn't the first time that necklace was stolen."

My brows rose. "What? When?"

"Fourteen years ago. Someone broke into the Cullens' city house. According to Dana, the necklace is an 18k white gold piece engraved with diamond cuts—just the chain is worth about three grand."

"Just the chain?"

He nodded. "And the pendant is a four-carat vintage sapphire from Sri Lanka. Lady Victoria was legit royalty, so the necklace has historical value, too."

"That sounds... very expensive."

"It is. Which is where the problem comes in. The necklace was insured—and when it was stolen, the Cullens got a $65,000 payout for it."

I stared. "Please tell me Lucy just lost a replica."

Logan lifted his hands. "Or... the Cullens committed insurance fraud. Once you get paid for an item, the insurance company technically owns it. If it shows up again, the claimant's supposed to repay the money or return the item."

I leaned in. "So Mrs. Cullens might have given Lucy a necklace she doesn't legally own?"

Logan nodded. "I really hope Lucy doesn't know. Because if she does, she's complicit."

My stomach twisted. Lucy had begged me not to involve the police.

"Do you have to report this?"

Logan exhaled hard, rubbing the back of his neck. "You know I do, Maggie."

I bit my lip, heart sinking. "But the wedding is tomorrow. If I don't find that necklace before then..."

Logan reached for my hand again, his voice softer. "I'm suspended thanks to Ben, and the necklace is currently lost, right? There's no need to file a report yet."

I nodded. "I'm going to talk to Mrs. Cullens and Lucy. I need answers."

Logan gave me a look—part admiring, part worried. Then his expression darkened.

"One more thing."

I tilted my head.

He looked me straight in the eye. "Stay away from Louis."

That caught me off guard. "Louis? Why?"

Bruno lifted his head too, as if echoing my surprise.

Logan didn't blink. "I don't trust him. Remember the piece of aper you found, and the phone that was supposedly Nico's?"

I leaned closer as my stomach seemed to shrink.

"Well, Tricia saw you talking to Louis at the dinner. She broke protocol to protect you."

"What is it?" I asked, my voice quieter than I expected.

Logan's expression was hard to read—somewhere between jealousy and deep concern. "The note had Louis's address in the city. And that phone? It wasn't Nico's. Ralph claims he's never seen it before. But want to guess the only number saved on it?"

A chill ran down my spine. I swallowed and forced my voice to come out steady. "Louis Cullens?"

Logan took a long breath and rested his hand flat on the table. "He looks clean on paper. No record. No obvious connections. But something about him doesn't add up."

It was hard for me to imagine Louis as a criminal—especially a dangerous one. But then again... wasn't charm one of a con artist's most effective weapons?

"Just trust me," Logan said, his tone low and tight. "Keep your distance until I know more."

Bruno, who had been quiet by my side,

shifted closer to Logan, as if he were silently agreeing.

"All right," I said slowly. "But you have to promise to tell me the second you find anything. Sandie's more involved with him than I am."

Logan nodded once, but his jaw tightened. "Yeah. But Sandie's not the one he's been flirting with."

This time, there was no mistaking the edge in his voice. It was jealousy. And—though it probably shouldn't—my heart felt oddly content at the sound of it.

"You'll be the first to know," Logan added as he stood. "Take care, Maggie."

Chapter 22

Sandie wasn't thrilled that I was about to derail the carefully planned rehearsal day—but frankly, I didn't care. It was time for some explanations and clarifications from the Cullens and the soon-to-be Cullens. Unfortunately, I needed Sandie to help me track them down.

Logan wasn't worried about keeping quiet for two more days. In contrast, my anxiety was escalating.

"Lucy is freaking out, Maggie," Sandie said as I pulled up to the rental house and parked. "I doubt she'll call Mrs. Cullens."

I didn't wait for her to finish before jumping out of the car. Bruno hopped out right behind me and stayed close, his ears twitching as he took in the unfamiliar surroundings. He sensed my tension—he always did.

"She better call," I muttered, marching toward the front steps. "Or I—"

"Margaret!" a voice cut in, making me jump.

Louis appeared suddenly in the doorway, and I instinctively stepped back, pressing a hand to my chest.

"Dear goodness, you scared me," I said, trying to steady my breath.

"I'm so sorry," he replied quickly. "I didn't mean to startle you."

He looked flustered, brushing a hand through his hair. For the first time since I'd met him, he seemed genuinely nervous.

"Aren't you staying for brunch?" Sandie asked, walking up beside me with far more composure than I felt. "It should be starting pretty soon."

Louis gave a tight smile. "Yes, I am—but I had to run out. You know, last-minute errands for Johnathan. Stuff he forgot."

Bruno tilted his head as he watched Louis speak, then stepped a little in front of me, his body tensing just slightly. It was subtle, but I noticed it. He didn't growl or bark—just positioned himself protectively.

Sandie didn't seem fazed by Louis's behavior. She breezed past him into the house. "I'm sure I'll be in that position soon," she said lightly.

Louis chuckled awkwardly and started walking toward his car. "Well, I'll see you soon," he said, offering a wave over his shoulder.

I watched him leave, Logan's voice ringing in my ears. Something felt off, and I didn't buy that his hurry was because of Johnathan.

However, before I could dwell on it, a sharp voice pierced the air from upstairs.

"Is she crazy? I'm not calling Dorothy!"

Lucy.

I glanced at Sandie, who had frozen just inside the doorway, her face a mask of patience. Bruno gave a small, sympathetic whine and leaned against my leg, grounding me in the moment.

Here we go.

Dorothy Cullens took over an hour to show up at the house—and only did so because

Johnathan called her twice. The second time, he'd threatened to elope.

Just like the day I first met her, she entered with perfect posture and an air of superiority. But unlike that day, there wasn't a trace of politeness on her face. This time, her expression brimmed with exasperation and anger.

"What could possibly be so urgent that I had to cancel my morning appointment, Johnathan?" she asked coldly, ignoring Lucy—who sat beside her son—and Sandie, who was waiting on the other couch.

She hadn't seen me.

Yet.

I stepped out from where I'd been standing near the wall, Bruno at my side. His ears perked up as the tension in the room rose.

"Care to explain how Lucy ended up taking photos with a necklace that was reported stolen fourteen years ago?"

Dorothy's face drained of all color. Her shoulders slumped, and for a moment, her mask cracked. She collapsed onto the couch beside Sandie. Johnathan let out a short, disbelieving laugh—until he looked at his mother. Then the humor disappeared from his face like a switch had been flipped.

"What is she talking about?" he asked, eyes

on Dorothy. When she didn't answer, he turned to me. "Where—where did you get this crazy idea? That necklace has been in my family forever! Ask Granny—she'll tell you the entire story—"

"I asked her," I interrupted. "I'm sure she has no idea about the robbery at your parents' property."

Johnathan stood up, clearly rattled. "What robbery? What are you talking about?"

For a moment, I doubted whether he knew anything about it. Johnathan wasn't exactly the world's best liar. His shock looked—and sounded—completely genuine.

Lucy's voice came next, soft but quickly rising. "How could it be stolen if it was in your house all this time?" Then realization hit her, and she gasped. "You gave me a fake—no. No, I know diamonds, and those were real. You recovered it but didn't say anything—this is fraud."

She turned to me, eyes wet and voice cracking. "I had no idea, Maggie. I swear to you. You have to believe me. Sandie, I promise—if I had known, I would never—"

Sandie shot to her feet. "That's why you didn't want to call the police? You lied, Lucy! You put my sister in danger!"

Tears streamed down Lucy's face. To my surprise, I found myself stepping in between them. I placed a gentle hand on Sandie's shoulder. "I really don't think she knew. Just look at her."

Lucy was crumbling—whatever part she'd played, she wasn't built for this level of deceit. And from what I could see, Johnathan wasn't either.

Bruno pressed gently into my leg, sensing the spike of emotions. His calm presence grounded me just enough to move toward Dorothy.

She looked like she wanted to sink right into the cushions and disappear.

"Care to explain?" I asked. "And maybe start with an apology."

Her eyes snapped to mine. "Apologize? To you?"

I shook my head and gestured toward the couple across the room. "To them. It's incredibly hypocritical to threaten Lucy over losing the necklace, just to keep yourself out of jail."

Dorothy's lips parted like she was going to argue—but instead, she sighed. Her hands covered her face for a beat, and when she finally looked up, the wrinkles around her eyes had deepened. Her shoulders sagged with the weight of years of secrets.

"I'm sorry for the drama about Julia's necklace," she muttered. "But this is exactly what I was trying to avoid."

I sat across from her, saying nothing. I didn't offer her an out. I wanted the full story.

Dorothy finally spoke, eyes on Johnathan. "It's true. Fourteen years ago, when we bought the chalet, someone broke in. They stole several things—including the necklace."

Johnathan's jaw clenched. His voice was cold. "And you didn't think to tell me?"

"You were nineteen, in college. Your father and I didn't want to worry you or your sister. Besides, we were fine. Your father called it a 'blessing in disguise.' The company had just lost investors, and the insurance payout helped him buy them out."

"A big problem when the necklace reappeared," I said evenly.

Dorothy turned to me—no longer angry, just tired. "A year later, our gardener found it behind a bush. I told Frank we should contact the insurance company, but he refused. Said the business couldn't afford to repay the money. So we didn't."

Lucy's eyes flared with disbelief. "But

you've had the means to pay it back for years. Why not come clean? Why not make it right? Now your son and I are part of this."

Dorothy's expression tightened. She ignored Lucy entirely and turned her gaze to Johnathan, then to me.

"I forgot about it. It didn't cross my mind again until Julia brought up the tradition before your sister's wedding. Frank didn't seem concerned, so I let it go. Then Julia started causing problems at the company because she didn't want me involved after your father died... All her will issues... It has never been important."

Her tone sharpened as she looked directly at Lucy. "It wouldn't be a problem if you hadn't shown up and lost it. Am I right?"

Lucy paled. She stepped back, but Johnathan reached for her hand and guided her toward the door. He stopped at the threshold, turned to his mother, and said in a voice that left no room for argument:

"Stay away from our wedding, Mother."

And with that, they were gone.

Bruno let out a quiet huff and walked over to me, resting his chin on my knee.

I stroked behind his ears and let the silence settle, heavier than before.

Chapter 23

"The problem is, none of this explains who stole it this time," I said to Sandie as we walked toward the entrance of the house.

Dorothy hadn't waited long after Johnathan left with Lucy. I actually felt sorry for her. She walked out of the room looking hurt—almost in tears.

"I assume Logan helped you figure all this out?" Sandie asked.

"He did," I said, lifting my shoulders in a shrug. "And he'll have to report it. But without the necklace, I'm not sure what that will accomplish. We have to find it before Logan goes back to work. And... I think we should give Dorothy a chance to do the right thing."

Sandie frowned and looked like she was

about to scold me when a voice snapped through the backyard.

"What the heck did you do?"

Before I knew it, Sandie was already storming toward the back deck. I rushed after her, just in time to stop her from opening the door all the way. We were on the second floor, and from that angle I couldn't see much, but the voices were unmistakable.

Louis.

And he did not sound happy.

"I told you not to—"

Another male voice interrupted him, calmer but firm. "It's done now. I told you I was going to fix it."

"You shouldn't have dragged her into this mess in the first place!" Louis snapped. "Whatever you did, you'd better stop. You're messing with my business—and you know that won't end well for you."

A rustling sound came from the bushes beneath the deck. The voices grew distant, too far away to understand. I backed away from the door and tiptoed to the hallway, trying not to let my heels betray me. A moment later, I heard a door downstairs slam shut.

"Fix it?" Sandie whispered behind me. "Do you think Theodore is trying to help Lucy?"

I turned. "Theodore? Are you sure that was him?"

Sandie nodded confidently. "Yes, with Louis. I've been here all week, and they're not exactly quiet."

"But why would Theodore want to help Lucy?" I asked. "Do you think she told him about the necklace?"

She thought for a second, then shook her head. "Actually, I don't think so. Lucy told me Theodore's been cold toward her lately. She said it hurt because he used to be the only one who openly welcomed her into the family."

Louis had said something like that when I met him. He also told me Julia had given a larger share of the will to Theodore—and Dorothy had just mentioned the will when talking about the fraud.

And Julia... she'd expressed concern about Theodore, too. Guilt could make people do strange things.

"If this is about the will," I said aloud, "then the root of it all has to be money."

I looked to Sandie. "Do you know if Julia's been having financial issues?"

She frowned, thinking hard—then suddenly snapped her fingers. "The assisted living!"

"Shhh!" I hissed, motioning for her to lower her voice. If we could hear voices from the first floor, so could they. "What about it?"

Whispering now, Sandie said, "Lucy told me Julia's not happy in her new place. Dorothy moved her out of the house a few months ago. Supposedly, doctors told Dorothy that Julia couldn't live alone anymore—and Dorothy refused to pay for private nurses."

"So Dorothy's paying Julia's bills?"

"I suppose so."

And just like that, everything started to fall into place.

Julia had tried to protect her wealth by giving it away before Dorothy could touch it. She'd made Theodore her main heir. He had seemed sincerely concerned about her the other night. And if Louis was telling the truth and Theodore had lost most of his inheritance... then he had a motive.

A big one.

"I think I know who took the necklace, Sandie," I said quietly, my pulse quickening.

Bruno, who'd been quietly shadowing us the whole time, perked up and let out a low whine—as if to say, *finally.*

Of course, things could never be easy.

By the time Sandie and I made it down-stairs, Theodore had vanished, and Louis claimed not to know where he'd gone. More importantly, Linda had called—twice—and made it very clear I'd better show up at the of-fice immediately.

So less than twenty minutes later, I was stepping out of the elevator on the third floor of City Hall. And even from that distance, I could sense the problem.

My mom was there.

And she was not happy.

"Come on, Bruno," I muttered, glancing at my faithful sidekick. He hesitated at first—smart dog—but eventually followed. "I know, she can be scary, but we've got this."

Linda stood at her desk, arms crossed and lips pressed in a line, nodding along with what-ever my mother was saying. That was even more worrying.

The moment my mom spotted me near the entrance, she raised her voice—loud enough to stop conversations across the office.

"What are you thinking?!"

From the corner of my eye, I spotted Bert, Terry, and Sophie attempting to disappear behind the far wall. Not that it mattered. They could hear everything.

Part of me wanted to yell right back—remind her that she was in my office and I wasn't a kid anymore. But instead, I turned toward my team and called out, loud enough for all to hear:

"Now you see where my personality comes from! So you'd better not make me mad."

That earned a few laughs and got people back to work. Even Mom seemed to tone it down, if only a little.

"We need to talk," she said, more tightly than before.

"So I heard." I gave Linda an apologetic smile, then led Mom into my office and shut the door behind us. Bruno padded in beside me and sat down stiffly at my side. His ears drooped, and his tail barely twitched. I wasn't sure if he was protecting me... or bracing for impact.

"Your sister is pregnant. Your daughter is five. Do you really think it's smart to involve them in a criminal investigation?"

I opened my mouth, but she steamrolled right over me.

"Margaret Willow, this is dangerous enough for you. And this one? These people aren't playing games. Two guards dead. Two more in the hospital!"

"What people?"

My mom threw up her arms and started pacing the tight space. "Don't pretend you don't know. Was this Logan's idea? Or was it yours? Did you decide to jump in after I told you about it?"

I took a long breath and worked hard to keep my voice even. Based on what Logan had told me, I could guess this had to do with Ben. But I needed to be sure.

"Logan didn't get me into anything, Mom. And if you're talking about the necklace—"

"Yes!" she shouted, loud enough that Bruno jumped and let out a small whimper. "The necklace, Maggie! And don't you dare deny it. I heard Sandie on the phone. She said you know who took it!"

I pushed my hair back and exhaled slowly. My patience was thinning.

"Did you ask Sandie about it?"

"I've been keeping an eye on you, Maggie," my mom yelled. Part of me understood some of Darcy's comments, but the other part was in denial. "You've been running around town, asking questions, and scheming with Logan! I know!"

My mom slammed a photo onto my desk. I had paid little attention to the museum piece she'd mentioned before, but now I had no choice. And wow... now I understood the obsession.

Unlike Lucy's necklace, which was already quite the showpiece, this one screamed wealth and power. The centerpiece stone was roughly the size of Darcy's fist, a deep green-blue framed in golden filigree. The elaborate chain curled into delicate leaves, each one inset with tiny blue gems.

"That looks heavy," I muttered, genuinely impressed.

My mom scoffed. "That's your concern? This thing is invaluable. And people have died for it."

I sighed, scrolling through my phone. "Yes, yes, you told me all about the curse."

"Margaret, I can't—"

I held up my phone, showing her the photo of Lucy wearing the Cullens necklace.

Her eyes narrowed. "What's this?"

"That's the necklace Sandie was talking about, Mom."

She took the phone from me, inspecting the photo carefully.

"It belongs to Johnathan's family. Someone stole it from Lucy the other day. That's what I'm looking into—and as you can see, it has nothing to do with whatever international jewel conspiracy you think I'm tangled in. I've also been dealing with a major issue involving the golf course and country club. That is part of my job."

My mom's cheeks flushed pink as she handed the phone back. "I thought you were— I mean, Ben caught Logan and Arthur in some kind of side investigation, and I assumed you were part of it... I'm sorry, Maggie."

I tapped my fingers on the desk and stared at her. "You told Ben about this."

It wasn't a question.

She nodded slowly, the guilt all over her face.

"Mom! You should've come to me first. You made things worse for Logan—and even Bruno paid for it."

"Bruno?" Her eyes widened, but when I said his name, my furry pal trotted over and rested his head gently on her lap.

"What happened to you, sweetheart?"

"He's suspended. Like Logan."

She rubbed behind Bruno's ears, her voice finally softening. "Well... maybe you both needed a vacation. If anyone asked me."

"Mom, that's not the point."

She lifted her hands in surrender. "I know, I know. And I *am* sorry. I'll talk to Ben. I'll apologize to Logan. But you can't blame me for worrying. You've been wrapped up in more crimes than I can count lately."

Just as I opened my mouth to respond— probably loudly—a knock at the door interrupted us.

"Sorry to interrupt," Linda said, her voice unusually clipped. "Pat called. There's a problem at the Country Club."

I groaned. Of course there was. "See my point?" I said to my mother. Grabbing Bruno's leash, I stood up and headed for the door.

"I'll see you at home, Mom. And stop gossiping around."

She opened her mouth to protest, but I was already gone, done with speeches and more than ready to be done with Pat and his golf drama.

Chapter 24

W hen I arrived at the golf course, I headed straight for the restaurant to make sure everything was running smoothly. At the entrance, I spotted Logan chatting with a golfer by the bar. The customers looked content, and the waitstaff moved efficiently through the space, so I shifted directions and made my way to the office.

"Pat better be there, Bruno," I muttered, stomping down the hallway, making the few golfers in the building step quickly out of my way.

His office door was closed, but voices inside drifted through. As I got closer, I began to make out the conversation.

"She'll be able to help you," I recognized Pat saying.

A barely familiar voice replied. "She hates me. And I don't blame her. You made a bigger mess out of all this."

"*Me?*" Pat raised his voice just as I pushed the door open without knocking.

"What mess did you make bigger this time, Pat?"

Pat startled, but I wasn't expecting Nico to scream and leap a foot into the air.

"Dear goodness, Maggie! Can you knock?" Pat scolded, while Nico stood with both hands over his chest, breathing heavily.

I didn't have time for drama. "Who were you talking about?" I asked Pat, stepping into the room.

He cleared his throat and moved toward his desk. "You, of course. The R-Parks Director."

Suspicion prickled at my neck. I scanned the office. "And since when do you need the R-Parks Director?"

Pat sighed and gestured for me to sit. In all the years I'd known him, he had never asked me to sit down. That alone was alarming. I settled into the chair, but let Bruno roam the office. Last time we were in a questionable situation, he'd found something I missed. I wanted to give him space—and watch him closely.

"Do you remember how I worked with a youth program in the city?" Pat asked. He nodded toward Nico. "My friend here was one of the kids in the program."

I looked at Nico, unsure where this was going. "Did you play in a city league?"

Nico nodded, but it was Pat who answered.

"He did. But that's not the point. The program I volunteered for was... well, a reintroduction to society."

I tilted my head. "A reintroduction?"

Nico shifted. "I got into a lot of trouble growing up. When I was under fifteen, I found myself in a... difficult situation. My family—" He sighed. "They're still my family, but I wanted to get away from their business."

A cold shiver ran down my back. I sat up straighter. "You mean... criminal?"

Pat cut in, "The less you know, the better, Maggie."

That did not reassure me. I discreetly wrapped my hand around Bruno's leash and slipped my phone from my pocket.

"Nico hasn't been involved in any crimes since he joined the league—decades ago. He's, what, ten, twelve years older than you? Played at your level back when he was your age."

I nodded but didn't relax. Not until Bruno came and sat beside me, calm and unbothered. That helped. A little.

"My family had an event business as a cover-up," Nico said.

"You told me you used to run your family business the day I met you," I said, careful to keep my anxiety from my voice.

Nico lowered his eyes and shook his head. "I'm sorry about that. I worked with my family for years. My dad taught me a lot of good... and not-so-good things. Big events, big money. Easy to manipulate numbers and stuff. I was good with that part. After juvenile detention, I moved to the city. With Pat's help, I worked a lot of events. More like private parties and weddings—away from my family. After years of trying, I even got my registration and license for it."

I pushed my hair back as the pieces began to click. "Your brother—he doesn't work with you, does he?"

Nico's face went pale. Pat answered.

"No. But now he's trying to force Nico back into the family business. That's why we need your help."

I pointed to myself. "Me? What can I possibly—?"

"Well, first, don't fire Nico over this," Pat said, lowering his voice. "And don't let him get pushed out after the wedding."

I opened my mouth, ready to argue, but Pat rushed on.

"The Mayor and Council came for breakfast after messing around on the driving range. They're thrilled you solved the issue and love the new folks running the restaurant. I'm sure they'll offer them the job permanently, which leaves Nico out—and puts him back in his brother's hands."

I stood and paced. The last thing I wanted was to be tied to a criminal family in any capacity. But I knew Pat. His pride would never let him risk the course—or his reputation—without cause. And I still remembered Nico falling unconscious... and Ralph. That memory sent chills up my spine.

"Did your brother push you down the stairs?" I asked.

Nico didn't answer, but the fear in his eyes said everything. I looked at Pat. "How would keeping Nico here drive his brother away?"

Nico stepped forward. "Ralph's been sabotaging every job I get. I'm sure he was the one who called my last client about my record. But here... well, you already know about me."

Pat nodded. "Exactly. Nico's family doesn't need him. They want to control him. If we give him a chance, I know he'll take it. He's been clean for years."

I let Bruno walk over to Nico. He wagged his tail and gave Nico a lick on the hand. That alone told me what I needed.

"You said you're good with numbers. Can you run the restaurant?"

Nico's face brightened. "I might need time to learn the place, but yes. I can handle the management side and the catering."

I turned to Pat. "If I agree to this, the Mayor and Martin have to know about Nico's background."

Pat rolled his eyes. "Then this is a waste of time. They'll never—"

"Do you believe in him or not?"

"I'm putting my job and reputation on the line for him, Margaret. *Of course* I believe in him."

"Then if you want my department's support, you need to change."

He frowned, but I didn't let him speak.

"First, stay away from anything related to

the restaurant. This isn't part of your contract and you know it."

"He was stealing from me!" Pat shouted.

"He wasn't," I snapped. "I had my department check. Everything was reported. But I can't blame him for doing things his own way —you don't make it easy to work with you, Pat. You're a bully."

"I am not!" he said, looking at Nico, who suddenly found the carpet very interesting.

"I don't need to ask him," I said firmly. "I've known you for years. I was your student."

"And you turned out to be a great golfer. See? It worked. Nico's all reformed thanks to my lessons."

"You're a great coach. A mentor, even. But that's not the issue. I'm talking about people who come to play golf for fun. You have to let them enjoy the game. If they want help, fine. If not, back off."

"Margaret! They're shaming this glorious game!"

I nearly laughed at his dramatic tone. "This is a public course, whether you like it or not. If you want Nico to get a second chance, you need to grow up and set the example."

Pat's eyes flashed with resistance as he took

a step forward, but Bruno calmly moved between us—alert and ready.

"This is my course. I should have the final say on everything. That caterer was a disaster—just imagine what we could've done better without them!"

"What's going on, Pat?" I asked, keeping my tone firm but calm. "You've got to stop trying to control everything. You're a fantastic golfer—but let the rest of us handle the club."

His expression shifted, softening with something closer to fear than pride.

"I may not be good for much longer," he admitted quietly.

Mr. Elliot's comment came to mind. "What do you mean? Talk to me. You're still my coach, you know."

Pat sighed. "I blew out my knee a year ago. I need a replacement." He spoke quickly, as if trying to get it over with. "I know it's a common procedure, and most people bounce back, but—this is my life, Maggie. You get it. I'm the great Pat Potter. I can't just... let it go."

Bruno trotted over and gently sniffed his hand. I understood. Losing what you know—what defines you—is terrifying.

"We'll figure it out," I said gently. "Just like you're giving Nico a second chance, you've got to give yourself one, too. Get the surgery. We'll make it work. You don't need to run the country club to matter. I'm not firing you. Maybe it's time to get back to coaching instead of yelling about how bad golfers are ruining the course."

Nico chuckled, and I smiled.

"Just promise me you'll keep an open mind and welcome everyone here—no more over-the-top criticism. Deal?"

Slowly, he nodded.

In the end, we spent the next hour working out details. I agreed to support Nico under one condition: someone else would oversee the restaurant and mentor him. Fortunately, that person was just a few steps away—currently manning the bar.

Logan was sipping something behind the bar when I walked in. I still felt bad about his arm, but it was nice to see him working somewhere that didn't put his life on the line.

I didn't love that my mom had made such a big deal over a misunderstanding, but I under-stood her point. No one wants to see their loved ones in danger. And by now, I couldn't deny that Logan was definitely in that category.

"I thought you'd left," he said as I leaned on the bar. "I was starting to worry you were mad at me or something."

Bruno had already made his way behind the bar and sat politely at attention, clearly hoping for a treat. Logan gave him a look and a muttered complaint, but walked over to give him a quick rub on the head anyway.

"I'm not mad at you," I said. "Though you might be a little mad at my mom."

Logan raised an eyebrow and smirked. "You could've warned me she was going to call. I seriously thought my time had come."

I laughed, imagining how that conversation had gone. Poor guy—my mom still had the power to rattle even the bravest detective.

"So what brings you here?" he asked, sliding a cold glass of iced tea in front of me. "Not that you need an excuse to check on your staff."

I glanced around the restaurant. Despite it being a weekday afternoon, a few tables were full and the servers moved smoothly between them. Pretty typical for a golf course.

"Pat wanted to talk," I said. "I think we figured things out."

I explained everything, watching Logan's face closely. As a police officer, I wasn't sure how he'd take it. But his first question surprised me.

"Do you believe Pat will actually keep his word and stay out of the country club's business?"

I sighed. "I hope so. Honestly, I think things wouldn't have gone this far if Troy had been a golfer. Pat just... sees the world through that lens. It's easier for me to get it now."

"Poor Pat," Logan said, shaking his head. "Does he know you'll be keeping tabs on him?"

"I think he figured it out. Though I'm pretty sure he's still not inviting me to play a round with him anytime soon."

Logan laughed, then stepped away to help a customer. When he returned, his expression had shifted—more serious.

"It's a good plan, but... I *do* believe in second chances, Maggie. I just don't like that Ralph is back in the picture. Would you mind if I asked Tricia to monitor him?"

Relief swept over me—more than I expected. I guess I wasn't entirely sure about Ralph either.

"That would be great," I said, then hesitated. "Actually... I need another favor."

Logan leaned on the bar with a warm smile. "Anything for you."

The room seemed to warm up with that one sentence, and I was sure he could read the blush on my face. I looked toward the door, trying to steady my breath.

"I agreed to close the entire facility this weekend and two days next week," I began. "But I was hoping you could work with Nico —help him learn how to run this place?"

Logan cleared his throat and gave the counter a gentle slap. "That's not exactly what I had in mind... but sure. Why the full closure?"

"Well, with the wedding, no one's really planning to play golf Saturday or Sunday. And we've been meaning to drain the ponds for cleaning—we figured we could get it done now instead of gambling on the fall weather. Plus, it'll be easier to train Larry, Felix, and Nico without a full crowd. Maybe just a few select guests."

Logan tapped his finger to his nose. "Smart. Let me guess—your 'select crowd' is the Council and your mom's friends?"

I chuckled. "Actually, it's more about making sure Ralph doesn't show up. I know a few days isn't much, but..."

Logan's expression shifted. The professional in him came forward.

"If he *does* show up," he said, "I'll be here. And I'll have a real conversation with Nico too. Sound good?"

Somehow, he always knew just what to say to make me feel better—at least until he added:

"So... what happened with Lucy's necklace?"

Probably, it wasn't the necklace that truly bothered me—it was the thought of heading into that rehearsal.

"That bad, huh?" Logan asked, reading my silence.

I laughed. "Not really. Actually, I think I know who took it. Want to hear my theory?"

Chapter 25

I made a mental note to call my friend Ella Sands and apologize for ever complaining about her wedding rehearsal. After two hours of repeating the same entrance, walking the same path, and posing for endless pictures, I was ready to lose my mind.

Worse, I hadn't had a chance to talk to Theodore. He wasn't paired with me—I was stuck with Louis—and the breaks weren't long enough to mingle.

"I think we've got it," Sandie finally said in a tone I knew well—and wouldn't dare argue with.

"I don't know, Sandie," Lucy replied. "Your part looks good, but I'm not sure the people in the back understand the importance of keeping time with the music."

Sandie turned around, and I could tell she had a few choice words she wasn't saying. Thank goodness the photographers stepped in.

"I have another wedding to get to," one of them said. "I'll see you all tomorrow—bright and early."

She didn't wait for Lucy's protests. Johnathan was left to soothe his bride-to-be, and the rest of the wedding party wasted no time heading toward the Grand Salon at the Country Club.

For a rehearsal, the room was already packed with guests I didn't recognize. The decorations were lovely, the tables beautifully set, and the food line well-organized. I felt a small wave of relief—Nico had done a great job, and so far, I hadn't seen Ralph anywhere.

A rich smell drifted in from the kitchen, promising a delicious dinner.

Sandie slipped her arm through mine and whispered in my ear, "Mrs. Cullens isn't here yet. Maybe you can talk to Theodore now. Lucy's freaking out—and not about the rehearsal."

I'd filled Sandie in earlier when I'd stopped home to change. My sweet sister had even brought a dress for me from the bridal shop. She knew my style well—soft lavender, a flowy skirt, pockets. No complaints there. The shoes, however, were another matter.

"Do you know where he is?" I asked, though I didn't need to. Sandie was already steering me through the crowd.

"He went to the bar a few minutes ago."

The bar wasn't far, but my shoes made the walk feel longer, louder, and more awkward than it needed to be. As we arrived, Louis emerged with a drink in each hand.

"My luck," he said, grinning. "I bump into the prettiest girls in the room, and I'm stuck playing delivery boy to my parents. Typical."

I smiled, about to reply, but Sandie breezed right past him into the restaurant.

"Are you mad at him?" I asked, noticing for the first time that she looked truly annoyed.

"No," she said curtly, pointing toward the bar. "There he is. He better still have it."

She marched straight toward Theodore, ignoring Logan, who gave her a wave, and Laura, one of the bridesmaids, who tried to ask her something about the wedding flowers.

"You stole the necklace from Lucy," Sandie said, loud enough to turn heads. "Where the heck did you put it?"

Theodore's face went pale. He crushed the

cup in his hand, and before I could move, he shoved Sandie. That was all it took.

Logan moved faster than I could blink, blocking his escape, and Bruno launched himself at Theodore, pinning him to the ground.

"Get it off me!" Theodore shouted. "I did nothing! Get it off!"

"Bruno," Logan commanded, pulling Theodore up with one hand and pushing him against the wall. Bruno stayed close, a low growl still rumbling in his throat.

"The necklace," I said, crouching nearby but keeping my distance. "Where is it? Did you sell it?"

Theodore's expression darkened, and his voice dropped. "It belongs to Granny. None of you have the right to it."

"I agree," I said. He looked surprised, but I didn't let him interrupt. "It belongs to her. So —did you give it back?"

He relaxed slightly, and Logan eased his grip, but Bruno didn't budge.

"She believes in me," Theodore said. "She always has. And I... I've lost everything. I wanted to help her. My ridiculous aunt shouldn't be deciding anything for her. Granny's still sharp. She should be the one making choices about her life."

He rested his elbows on his knees and lowered his head.

I sighed and closed my eyes for a moment. "You tried to sell it."

"No!" he snapped. Then, quieter, "Well... yes. But I couldn't. Louis's guy didn't want it, so I took a picture to a pawn shop and..."

His eyes filled with anger.

"He told me it was marked. Like stolen merchandise. You see? My aunt committed fraud with my grandmother's heirloom. And now I can't even use it to help her."

I wanted to point out that if it was such a treasured possession, maybe trying to sell it wasn't the way to help. But that wouldn't get the necklace back.

"Where is it now?"

"Did you hear me? My aunt committed fraud—"

I moved closer and lowered my voice. "I heard you. And he heard you," I said, gesturing to Logan. "He's a police officer. If your aunt committed fraud, she'll face consequences. But we need the necklace."

"Not here," Logan said firmly. "Too many people. Let's take this to the office."

Theodore didn't try to run. He just collapsed onto Pat's couch, defeated. Logan shut the office door behind Sandie, who slipped in quietly, and Bruno trotted in behind her, tail low and ears alert as if sensing the weight in the room.

I didn't waste any time. "Where is the necklace, Theodore?"

His eyes stared into the distance. His hair was a mess, his tie was crooked, and the desperation on his face felt like a whole new person. Bruno padded forward and sat at my feet, watching Theodore carefully.

"It was Louis's idea... well, kind of."

"Louis Cullens?" Logan asked.

"Yes, Johnathan's cousin," Sandie answered, settling into one of the chairs. "He's the one running most of the family business."

Logan glanced her way. "Do you think he knew about the fraud?"

She shrugged and looked at me. "I don't know. I think only Mrs. Cullens knew. But... Louis is smart. He could've figured it out."

Theodore cut in, his tone tinged with a

strange admiration. "If he knew, he would've done something. He hates my aunt."

"You said he had a guy and that it was his idea," Logan said. "Sounds to me like Louis knew more than you think."

Theodore shook his head violently, his hair flopping in every direction. His voice rose, edged with panic.

"No, no—his friend's a geologist or something. I asked Louis if he knew someone who could help me appraise a gem. He thought I meant my mom's engagement ring. He had no idea about the necklace. And when I said it was his idea... it wasn't on purpose. I overheard him and one of his buddies talking about how things disappear out here. Phones, wallets, golf balls. I just thought..."

He looked at me, eyes pleading.

"I thought it could work."

"What could work?" I asked, already feeling the pit forming in my stomach.

"The pond," he said. "The one on the course. They were saying how no one ever finds anything in there—I figured... I figured if I tossed it in..."

I closed my eyes. I could still hear Pat talking about draining the ponds.

"You threw the necklace in the pond?"

Theodore pressed his lips together and nodded.

That was it. I lost every ounce of patience and grabbed his collar, pushing him back against the couch cushions. Bruno leapt to his feet and stood at my side, tense and ready, watching Theodore with sharp eyes.

"Which pond? Which hole?"

Logan stepped up and gently pulled me back by the waist as Theodore shouted,

"I don't know! Hole nine, I think. The one by the bridge? Maybe."

Logan steadied me and met my eyes.

"We'll find it, Maggie. I'm terrible at golf. I've dropped stuff in those ponds before, but you can get it back." He glanced down. "Bruno has helped me before. That's probably how he learned to retrieve."

Bruno's tail swished once at his name, and I looked down at him, the realization striking.

"I'm draining the ponds tomorrow. Before the wedding."

From across the room, a sharp cry cut through the moment.

Sandie.

I turned just in time to see her doubling over, clutching her belly, tears streaking her cheeks.

"Sandie!" I rushed to her side, Bruno right beside me. "Is the baby coming?"

She shook her head, but her face was pale and her voice barely came out.

"My heart—" she gasped. "I can't breathe—"

Logan was already in motion. He pressed a phone into my hand and helped ease Sandie to the floor, careful and calm. Bruno lay down at her side, resting his head lightly on her thigh.

"It's going to be okay," Logan told her, voice steady.

I didn't need him to spell it out. I dialed 911, and for the second time that summer, I found myself explaining a medical emergency to an operator—this time, with my heart lodged firmly in my throat and my sister's hand clutched tightly in mine... and Bruno quietly standing guard beside us.

Chapter 26

Apparently, putting your legs up while pregnant helps slow your heartbeat. Thanks to Logan, by the time the ambulance arrived, Sandie's color had returned and she was breathing steadily again. Bruno sat by her side the entire time, ears alert, resting his chin next to her as if he knew she needed comfort more than anything.

While we waited, I called Paul and sent him straight to the hospital—there was no point in him trying to reach the country club. By the time the paramedics came in and did their quick evaluation, Sandie was stable, but they still loaded her gently onto a stretcher.

As they rolled her toward the door, I noticed she was holding Logan's hand tightly.

"He can't go with you," I said, stepping up. "I'll ride with—"

But Sandie shook her head and tugged Logan closer. "You have to help Lucy."

"Are you sure?" I asked, already feeling the protest rising in my throat.

"I'll be fine. I'm just tired and very pregnant. But Lucy's not okay. If she doesn't have that necklace tomorrow, Mrs. Cullens is going to shred her."

I rolled my eyes and shook my head, but of course she ignored me entirely.

"I'll take Logan with me," she added, shooting him a sideways look that clearly surprised him. "And after I yell at Paul for not being here, I'll send Logan back. Deal?"

Logan gave me a small smile, patting Sandie's hand. "Sounds like a plan," he said, though his voice didn't match his words, and his eyes gave away his unease.

He leaned toward me and lowered his voice. "Tricia's here. I saw her parked out front."

That was all he had to say. I nodded. Message received.

Bruno walked beside me as we watched the ambulance pull away, tail low but steady, as if he knew something big still hung in the air.

Of course, Theodore had used the chaos to make himself scarce—but I didn't need him anymore.

"Come on, Bruno," I said, clipping on his leash and rubbing his head. "Looks like your nose is up next. Let's go find a necklace."

I walked straight to hole seventeen instead of hole nine. Louis and his friends were right—plenty of things got lost in those waters. But Theodore wasn't a golfer. I remembered from my days playing this course that people often confused those two ponds and reported missing items in the wrong spot.

The daylight was fading by the time I reached the bridge, and most golfers had already moved past this part of the course. A good thing—no risk of a stray ball smacking me in the head.

"Let's check up here, Bruno," I said, leaning over to get a better view of the water.

If I'd had any doubt that the ponds needed to be cleaned, it vanished in that moment. From up on the bridge, I could see an unbelievable amount of weeds and muck—plus countless golf balls, soda cans, bottles, and even the occasional forgotten cooler.

"Kind of disgusting," I muttered to Bruno as we stepped off the bridge. "The good news? I know this pond isn't deep."

The shoreline was uneven, with several sloping spots that dropped into river rocks at the bottom. I sat down and pulled off my shoes, tying up the hem of my dress as high as I dared. Glancing around to make sure no one was watching, I sighed. I must've looked like a lunatic—barefoot, hiking up a dress, and about to wade into a man-made swamp.

I wished I had something that belonged to Julia or Lucy. Not that I knew how to explain to Bruno what to sniff for, but it looked so easy in the movies. I made a mental note to ask Logan how he actually trained Bruno. In the meantime, I worked with what I had. I un-clasped a silver necklace Sandie had given me and held it out.

"Here, Bruno," I said, showing him the chain in my hand. "We need to find something like this."

He leaned forward and sniffed it carefully. I gave him a few more seconds, then pointed to-ward the water. "Go fetch."

Bruno sat down and looked up at me.

I rolled my eyes and held the necklace out again. "Come on, buddy."

This time, I gently tossed the necklace just far enough to land in the shallow water.

"Go fetch!"

Bruno perked up, stepped forward, and dipped his snout into the pond. He came back with the necklace delicately held in his mouth.

"Good boy!" I beamed, petting him and taking the chain back. "You're amazing."

Only the faint lights from the country club and a rising moon lit the scene now—not exactly ideal conditions. I kissed the necklace, knowing full well I might lose it this time, and threw it deeper into the pond.

"Go get it!"

Bruno leaped in, tail wagging, splashing through the reeds. After a few moments of rooting around, he surfaced again, silver chain gleaming between his teeth.

"Good boy!" I said, giving him a bigger rubdown.

He rewarded me by shaking his entire muddy body, soaking me head to toe.

"Bruno!" I cried, wiping muck from my face, but he looked proud of himself. He was right, though—we didn't have time to complain.

I grabbed the necklace and prepared to throw it again, but this time I only faked the toss.

"Go get it!"

He darted into the pond anyway, nose low, cutting through the weeds like a pro. He dunked his head once, twice—each time adjusting course, sniffing the water.

He was nearly in the middle when he paused and plunged deeper.

Just then, I heard the crunch of brush behind me. I turned, heart jumping, but it was too dark to see anything clearly beyond a few feet.

Water splashed behind me. I whirled back in time to see Bruno leap through the reeds and land at my feet. Something dangled from his mouth—he'd found something.

Before I could grab it, a flashlight flared in my eyes, blinding me.

"I wasn't expecting you to make our job harder," a voice drawled. I recognized it immediately—Louis. "But then again, I wasn't expecting you to retrieve our treasure for us."

Bruno growled, deep and low, a moment before launching toward Louis's voice. At the same time, something hit my foot. Louis cursed. Bruno snarled and thrashed like he was in the middle of a fight.

I crouched down and saw something glinting near my foot. Only when I grabbed it did I recognize the cold and wet texture of metal—a necklace.

"Get off me, you monster!" Louis shouted, followed by a high-pitched yelp.

"Bruno!" I called, scrambling to my feet. A tall figure stood up in front of me. Without thinking, I grabbed my shoe and swung hard, smacking the figure square on the head. "Bruno, come!"

Bruno darted toward me, leaping over a crumpled body. I prayed I hadn't just killed someone.

I bent down to grab my other shoe—only to freeze. A few feet from the guy I just hit lay Louis.

I didn't wait. Clutching both shoes, I ran toward the country club. But something felt wrong. I'd never been faster than Bruno before. He was barely keeping up.

I stopped and turned. He limped behind me, and when I touched his front leg, he flinched. My fingers came away wet—and I hoped it was just pond water.

"Come on, handsome," I said, slowing my pace. "We're almost there."

As we made our way down the hill, the heaviness on the right side of my dress set alarms off in my head. I reached into the pocket and my fingers brushed the cold metal again.

The large gemstone on the necklace in my hand caught the weak light of the country club. My mother's explanation suddenly came to mind as I stared at the dark crystal transforming into a bright red one.

It wasn't Lucy's necklace.

It was something far more valuable.

Something worth stealing.

Something worth killing for.

Chapter 27
Friday, Night time...

And this was how I got tangled up in everything. I hadn't meant to get involved in a heist—especially not this one. My only goal had been to find Lucy's necklace. I had failed catastrophically, and now I needed to find a way to survive—and save Lucy at the same time.

"Hurry up!" Ralph barked, making Lucy yelp when he shoved the barrel of his gun into her back.

The music from the reception was loud enough that no one outside the course would hear us. The people who might've noticed my absence were no longer at the party, and I had no clue where Tricia had been—or if she had seen me.

"The police are here," I said, hoping to rattle him.

Ralph just laughed.

"That's good," he said, glancing over his shoulder with a smug grin. "They'll find Louis knocked out on the course—attacked by a K9 officer—and they'll figure out what happened."

Lucy's voice trembled. "What... what happened?"

Ralph stopped at the top of a small hill between holes one and nine, just behind the country club.

"How Louis killed you two when he decided to make a run for the necklace," Ralph said, his tone slick with malice. He looked at me with a smirk that sent a chill through my spine. "I got real mad when I heard your stupid plan to drain the ponds," he added, leveling the gun at me. "I was gonna kill you then. But now..." He shoved Lucy, and she stumbled, falling hard near the green's flagpole. "Now, that draining plan is the perfect cover. Louis kills you both here, grabs the necklace, your dog takes him down, he hits his head on a rock... you know the rest."

"You... you killed Louis?" Lucy sobbed.

Ralph crouched beside her and whispered

near her ear, "He wasn't part of the family, sweetheart."

The way he moved shifted the shadows just enough for moonlight to hit the green. I realized I was standing near a sand trap. Faking a trip over my dress, I fell onto the sand.

"For the love of—" Ralph grumbled, stalking toward me.

He didn't expect the cloud of sand I flung in his face.

"You little—!"

I didn't wait for him to finish. Grabbing the broomstick used for smoothing traps, I swung hard, catching him square on the side of the head. Ralph collapsed face-first.

I scrambled out of the trap and helped Lucy up.

"He killed—" she started to say, but then screamed.

A gunshot cracked through the air. I dropped instantly, pulling Lucy down with me.

"How could you?" Ralph shouted, clutching his leg.

I looked up and saw Nico standing over him, holding a gun with both hands. Just behind him, I spotted Larry and Felix running toward us.

"Don't move," Nico said in a voice I had

never heard before. Low. Cold. Dangerous. The kind of voice passed down in families where crime was part of the legacy. "It ends now."

Felix dropped to his knees beside us. "Are you two okay?"

Lucy nodded shakily.

"There's a man down by the bridge," I said.

Felix nodded, but it was Larry—shining a flashlight—who answered.

"Another one?"

"Another—?"

He pointed toward the country club. In the distance, I saw Louis sitting on the ground with his hands behind his back. Tricia was walking toward us with purpose. So Louis was not dead—just arrested.

"Just that one," I said, finally exhaling.

Nico lowered his gun only after Tricia reached us and cuffed Ralph. Not far behind her, I saw Bruno limping toward me, his ears low and his tail wagging weakly.

"Oh, Bruno," I whispered, rushing toward him and dropping to my knees to hug him tight.

He licked my chin once and rested his head on my shoulder, whining softly.

"I'm not a vet," Tricia said, crouching beside us, "but I think he'll be okay. He cut his paw on this—got tangled up in it."

She held up something I could barely make out, but Lucy gasped and lunged to grab it.

"My necklace!" she said, holding it close like a lost treasure.

I reached into my pocket and pulled out the other necklace. Heavy and cool in my palm, the stone in the center shimmered as I tilted it, unable to resist the temptation. It shifted colors once again, from greenish-blue to a deep reddish hue. This time, I had more time to admire it.

"Wow," Tricia murmured, leaning in for a closer look. "That is something."

Lucy stepped closer, still cradling her own necklace. "That's an alexandrite—one of the rarest and most expensive gemstones in the world."

"I guess my mother was right about the curse," I said, as Tricia pulled Ralph to his feet.

"Curse?" Lucy asked, but before I could answer, she added, "You shouldn't mess with that stuff. Just in case."

I tilted the necklace one more time and wished Darcy could see it. I'd never been big on gemstones, but I'll admit—handing that one over to the police stung a little.

Bruno whimpered beside me again, resting his head in my lap. I gently stroked his wet, muddy fur and whispered, "You did it, buddy. You saved the day."

He wagged his tail and let out a tired, content huff.

Epilogue

Lucy ran to me and gave me another hug after the first dance was done, then walked me to the side.

"I know I'm going to love baby Leslie, but I'm not happy she stopped her mommy from being at my wedding."

She didn't let me answer and grabbed my hands. "Thanks for filling in, though. I know I can be a lot, but... I owe you all my happiness, Maggie. Now, Johnathan and I will be fine."

I looked to the other side of the room, where the groom stood talking to his friends, silently hoping Dorothy would keep her word and repay the insurance. If not, pressing criminal charges against your mother-in-law doesn't exactly lead to a peaceful family dynamic. I couldn't blame Lucy for keeping the necklace as leverage. The more time I spent with her and the Cullens, the more I appreciated my own family.

"I'm just glad everything is over," I said honestly, which made her laugh. She wasn't so bad when she wasn't in panic mode.

"You really don't like weddings, do you?"

I wanted to say it was more the bride than the wedding, but instead, I sighed and lifted my shoulders.

"He should be ashamed of what he did," she said, and when I followed her gaze, I found Logan.

Now, I probably owed him more than one favor. After Sandie had to pull out of the wedding, Paul didn't hesitate to back out as well—a smart move, since Lucy tried to draft him to replace Louis. Long story short, she swallowed her pride and asked Logan to step in. I had a feeling he did it to finally bury the wedge between them. The reason didn't matter. I was just glad he had been with me through the hours of photos, the ceremony, and every other moment Lucy had planned.

Because of what he did, I wasn't going to let her speak badly of him. Not again.

"I think you should—" I started, but she kept talking like I hadn't even opened my mouth.

"Logan is a great guy. I knew I wasn't the person he wanted around when he found out about his parents, and that hurt me. Maybe one day I'll apologize to him. But to you—I'm sorry, Maggie. I knew he was your friend, and it wasn't my intention to mess that up. I truly thought he'd keep talking to you." One corner of her mouth lifted. "I should've known better. He was always a gentleman. He wouldn't get you in trouble."

My mind went blank. The only thing I managed was an awkward "Thank you."

Then she added, "I miss kissing him."

"You miss what?" I asked out loud, which made her chuckle and lightly push me.

"Oh, come on. It's normal to compare your boyfriends... or ex-husbands. I love Johnathan, but Logan was a way better kisser. You should try it."

My face turned red—a telltale sign of guilt. Thank goodness Lucy didn't notice and changed the subject.

"Your team did an amazing job at the golf course," she said, pointing toward the window that looked out over the fairway. "I had my doubts when you said you were draining the ponds. I mean, who does that before a wedding? But you were right—you can't even tell there was heavy machinery there."

"Thank goodness I know how to do my job," I replied, with sarcasm that flew right over her head.

"Everyone was disappointed the ponds didn't hide more treasures, though."

Johnathan came over and offered his arm. "We have to greet some guests. Sorry, Maggie."

I smiled, relieved to be rescued from a potentially awkward conversation. After all, we'd put his cousin in jail and placed his mother in a very peculiar situation.

"Mrs. Willow," Nico said as I reached the dessert table. "I just wanted to thank you for the opportunity. For believing in me."

He kept his eyes down and his voice low. "I know my family can be... intense, and—"

"Nico," I said, touching his arm, "you saved my life. I'm just glad everything seems to be working out. Hopefully, next week will help you settle in with Larry and Felix."

Pat walked up behind him and patted his back. "Told you he was a keeper."

"He may be, but you still have to keep your word."

Pat crossed his heart with a big grin. "I never break my word. And to prove it, I just sent an invitation to the R-Parks Department to form a foursome and come play this summer. On me."

Part of me wanted to check the email, but that would have been rude—and it would've stopped him from making his next statement.

"I may have suggested they make sure their director comes along. That'll increase their chances of winning."

"Pat! Not everything is about winning."

He winked, then snuck off with a plate stacked too high with cupcakes and cookies, tossing over his shoulder, "It isn't about winning. It's about getting my best student back on the course."

Nico shrugged. "I'm sure he isn't talking about me."

"Ready for Monday?" Logan asked as he approached the table, grabbing a cookie while keeping his other hand in his pocket.

According to him, while at the hospital with Sandie, his doctor happened to see him and cleared him for work, even removing the sling. Personally, I imagined Logan tracking down the doctor himself just to get cleared.

I wasn't going to complain. It really was good to see him back to normal. Even though Ben docked ten of his suspension days, meaning Logan only had Monday and Tuesday left to help at the restaurant.

"I'll be here bright and early," Nico said, taking an empty tray and using it as an excuse to leave.

"I think he's scared of you," I said to Logan, watching the new country club manager zigzag through the dancing crowd.

"That's a good thing," Logan replied, stepping closer. "That puts us on the same level."

I frowned and crossed my arms. "He's not scared of me."

Logan chuckled, then offered his hand, palm up. "Want to get out of—"

The music shifted from a modern pop tune to something classic, something out of Hollywood's golden age.

"Would you care to join me for this?"

I wasn't much of a dancer, and I was more than ready to leave, but I couldn't say no to the spark in his eyes or the playful smirk on his face.

I took his hand and let him lead me a few steps onto the dance floor. As soon as his feet touched the wood, he gave my hand a tug, spinning me toward him. I didn't need instructions. I placed my other arm around his neck, ready this time for the flutter in my stomach when his hand rested on my lower back and he guided us into the rhythm.

"Logan," I said, waiting for him to look down at me. "Thank you again for helping at the restaurant."

He smiled. "Not a problem. I should thank you for involving me in the necklace case. Although, I might be a little upset that you solved the big heist, too. Very sneaky."

I shook my head, smiling. "That wasn't part of the plan. Just like I'm sure you didn't expect to be with Sandie during Leslie's birth."

He stopped for a second and stared at me. "I wasn't there when Leslie was born. Paul made it just in time." He shook his head and started moving again. "Thank goodness for that."

I laughed. "Believe me, Paul is very thankful too."

I took a deep breath and bit my lip. I wanted to thank him for setting aside his issues with Lucy, but somehow that felt too hard to say.

"What is it?" he asked, a mix of curiosity and concern in his voice—just like what I felt inside.

"Thanks for being here with me."

His smile deepened as he leaned in, close to my ear. "I told you, Maggie. I'd do anything for you."

Bruno, who had been lying near the dessert table, stood up and gave a single low bark, as if to remind us he was still watching. Logan chuckled and reached down to scratch behind his ears.

"All right, partner," he said to Bruno. "We won't keep you waiting too long."

Bruno sat and gave a small tail wag, clearly approving.

For once, the three of us were exactly where we needed to be.

To Be Continued...

I hope you enjoy the book. If you want to receive updates from future books, behind the scene happenings and short puzzle mysteries, join The Detective's Dispatch group here.

Click here if you want to check out more books from Montie Red .

Author's Note

While the heirloom in *Cake, Vows and Extortion* is a work of fiction, some elements in this story were inspired by real events. During and after World War II, millions of valuable items—works of art, family heirlooms, jewelry, and personal treasures—were stolen, lost, or hidden as families fled persecution, especially Jewish families targeted by the Nazi regime.

The journey to return these stolen pieces has spanned generations. Museums, governments, private collectors, and descendants around the world continue to search for and restore these objects to their rightful heirs. Some stories have bittersweet endings. Others remain open mysteries.

In this book, I wanted to honor the quiet weight of memory that some families carry—

and the moral courage it takes to confront the past with empathy and truth.

Thank you for reading, for caring, and for joining me in unraveling this fictional mystery with real echoes from history.

Montie Red

Acknowledgments

For your patience, support, belief in the cause, staying with me and tolerating the time that I took away from all of you to sit down and write. During these years, I learned so much from all of you. For listening to my stories, complaints, and successes. For your help and critiques, for all of these and more,

To Each one of you, who loves to read mysteries and took the time to read my take on them. My amazing coaches; Scarlett and Bryan, my mystery group friends, Mom, Gloria, Teddy, Josephine, and You up there...

Thank you.

About the Author

Hi, I'm Montie Red, and I have a not-so-secret addiction to crafting twists, turns, and mysteries best solved with a cup of tea (or maybe a snack). My *R-Parks Mysteries* series is inspired by my love for quirky small-town charm, meddling sleuths, and the occasional murder that needs unraveling—purely fictional ones, of course!

My biggest motivation is my amazing daughter, who keeps me inspired and grounded. We share our home with two lovable dogs, five chatty birds, and a husband who frequently attempts daring escapes from my writing world—usually by pretending there's a very important game to watch or a mandatory tee time.

When I'm not diving into cozy mysteries, I step through portals to other worlds, writing sci-fi and fantasy adventures under the pen name Monica Red. Whether it's catching a killer or navigating interstellar chaos, I'm always in the thick of an exciting tale.

Thanks for joining me on this storytelling journey. Grab a cozy blanket, dive into a book, and let's solve some mysteries together!